BLACKWOODS:
THE BEGINNING

THE BLACKWOODS SERIES

Blackwoods: The Beginning
Blackwoods: The Blades of Redwater
Blackwoods: The Outcast of Azmar

OTHER BOOKS BY TERESSA J. MARTIN

Livskraft
Jorda

BLACKWOODS:
THE BEGINNING

TERESSA J. MARTIN
&
ADALINE MCMILLAN

To Mike Head,

Rest in peace. Know we always hold

you close to our hearts.

"This is your world
You're the creator
Find freedom on this canvas
Believe, that you can do it,
'Cuz you can do it.
You can do it."

-Bob Ross

PROLOGUE

THE MAN WALKED BRISKLY TOWARDS THE PLACE he was being drawn to. The place he'd left his family for. That thought caused pain to rise in his chest. He wanted nothing more than to be with his wife and daughter, but the pull to this place was too strong to ignore. He didn't want it to be, but he couldn't help it.

He knew when he met the boundary. When he crossed it, he fell to his knees, pain shooting through his head. His eyes burned like they were on fire. His pulse sped up and sweat broke out all over his skin as power radiated from him. He did his best not to scream, but he wasn't successful. As quickly as the pain had come, it left. He stayed crouched on the ground, trying to catch his breath. His eyes were still tingling, and his skin felt more sensitive than ever before. When he finally opened his eyes, he saw some residual glow that he couldn't explain. He blinked a few times, and it disappeared. He didn't trust himself to stand. Not yet. So he just looked around. Nothing looked different, even though he knew he'd generated some kind of magical barrier. It felt different, though. The trees were humming with energy, and the ground seemed to beg him to keep going.

Finally, he rose to his feet and started stumbling forward. His legs could barely hold his weight, but he kept going. He had to keep going. Before long, he was worried he'd never make it when the sight of the tree in front of him took his breath away. He'd never seen a tree so big, and he wasn't sure that another one existed. It seemed to go on forever. How had he not seen it above the canopy before? He took a step closer and was suddenly knocked back by a wave of power. He slammed into the tree behind him, falling to the ground. Another wave knocked his head into the trunk, causing him to black out for a moment. He slumped to the forest floor, heart pounding, the sound of blood rushing in his ears. Finally, after a few long minutes, the power stagnated. It was still there, but it wasn't knocking into him in steady beats of agonizing pain.

Cautiously, he rose to his feet, his breathing heavy and uneven. For some reason, he had the strangest urge to touch the tree in front of him. He didn't think that touching such a thing would be a good idea, but there wasn't a cell in his body that seemed to care. Against his better judgement, he kept going until his shaking fingers brushed against the rough bark.

He'd thought creating the barrier hurt, but it was nothing compared to this. Pain flowed through his entire body as the tree started to fall into the ground. He would have been amazed, but he was busy trying not to pass out. It picked up speed as it descended until the tree was completely gone. Silence fell over the forest, and he was left panting with the very distinct feeling that this wasn't over.

He was right. Out of the massive hole in the ground, wooden planks started to unfold and create a floor underneath him. Despite the pain, he managed to jump to his feet and look around, wonder sparking in his eyes. The floor that had formed was a perfect circle. Once it was complete, cabins started to build themselves, encircling the courtyard. The cabins were perfect spheres, something he'd never thought possible. Once they were perfectly formed, a circular wooden slab rose out of the ground in the very center of the courtyard, just where the tree had disappeared to. Around it, a perfectly smooth bench spun up from the ground, encircling the table.

Finally, the forest fell quiet.

ONE

CLAIRE DARTED THROUGH THE WOODS, branches snapping beneath her feet. She couldn't believe how clear the air felt, and she couldn't believe what she was seeing. She never imagined that trees would be so tall and so green, with bark that was almost black. Green wasn't a color Claire saw very often. In her home city of Everton, everything was in shades of gray. As she ran, she came to a clearing, her heart skipping a beat when she saw what was before her. Right in front of her was the most beautiful thing she'd ever seen. It was a magnificent waterfall that spilled into a lagoon. The clean scent from the water was almost as overwhelming as the color. It was an ethereal blue that was almost hard to look at. Even so, Claire couldn't bring herself to look away. In that moment, she wanted nothing more than to stay there forever. Somehow, she knew that lagoon was something special. It wasn't just the way the water glittered in the sunlight; it was the way it felt. The energy around it was so enticing, like she was home.

When Claire's eyes snapped open, she was breathing heavily, and her heart was racing. It was as though she'd actually been there. What was that place? That certainly didn't feel like a dream. It felt real. She shook her head and placed her hand over her heart, almost to make sure it was still there. It felt like it, sure, but would it ever feel normal again? Eventually, her heart slowed to its regular pace, and her lungs felt like they were processing oxygen again. She was inexplicably light-headed, and during that day, she couldn't really think straight. Her mind was on one thing.

She wondered if she'd ever have this dream again.

She wasn't disappointed when the dream continued every night until it went on for years. Now, she groaned out her frustration every time she woke. She'd had this dream for so long now, but she didn't know what it meant. It sounded crazy, but she knew it wasn't just a dream. It felt more like a premonition, like something inside her was trying to break free. She just didn't know what it was. Besides, at this point she was wondering if that notion was just wishful thinking. She got out of bed and readied herself for the day ahead. Not that her days were ever interesting. Still, she knew that today was different. Something was going to happen. At least, she hoped so, anyway.

She exited her bedroom through the sliding door and went down the plain hallway that led to the mess hall. Everything in the orphanage was boring and drab. The walls and floors were a slick white surface that was a stark reminder of how lonely she truly was. After her parents died, she'd been shipped to one of the many orphanages in Everton. Everton was a place of abundance—the richest city in the world, in fact—but you'd never know it by looking at the place. Sure, it was luxurious by global standards, but to the rest of Everton it was the picture of poverty.

Finally, Claire made it to the spiral staircase that led to the second floor. When she got to the top of the stairs, she was half tempted to throw herself over the railing.

"I'm so glad you're awake!" Beth shouted with excitement.

It's not that there was anything *wrong* with Beth per se, but she was quite annoying. Her blue eyes were dull and her dirty blonde hair looked like it needed to be washed. Her wide smile displayed white teeth, with the front two sticking out a little too much.

Instead of responding politely, Claire brushed passed her. Would it have been nicer to greet Beth in kind? Yes. However, Claire didn't think she had it in her to do so. Consequently, she chose to stay quiet. Unfortunately, Beth just scrambled along behind her like a lost puppy. Really, that was a perfect description of Beth. At fourteen, she was two years younger than Claire, and her parents had died only a year prior. A lot of the kids whose parents died when they were older became quite clingy. They just didn't know how to deal with their newfound loneliness. Claire didn't blame Beth, she just wished she'd find someone else to bother.

Claire did her best to ignore her as she ate, but Beth kept chattering away. Rubbing her temples, Claire finally met her eyes.

"I'm sorry, I really am. But I can't handle this right now. I'm just going through some stuff and…"

Beth's pleasant expression turned dark in the next instant. Her chin jutted out defiantly as she crossed her arms over her chest.

"I just wanted a friend," she spat.

Claire just stared at her, one eyebrow arched. With a sputtered curse, Beth took her tray and retreated to another table. Thank Heavens.

Just as Claire was starting to appreciate the silence, Mary, the madame of the orphanage, entered through the double doors. Her eyes locked onto Claire almost immediately, and a sigh left Claire's lips. She held a very special distaste for this woman and her arrogance.

"Claire, there's a visitor for you," she bellowed throughout the hall.

The teenager furrowed her brow in disbelief. Claire never had any visitors, and she didn't know who would visit her in the first place. She didn't know anyone on the outside. Not anymore.

"Is this a joke?" she asked, incredulous.

Mary frowned, her long, pointed nose tilted upwards. "Follow me," she demanded.

Claire rose from her seat, leaving her tray for someone else to take care of. She followed Mary to the front of the complex, somewhere she hadn't been since her parents' death. An incredibly tall man dressed in a long, navy over-coat with a silver shirt underneath was standing by the doors, his shoulders thrown back. As she got closer, she realized he was at least a foot taller than her, and she wasn't short by any means. She couldn't believe her eyes. She hadn't seen someone dressed like that in years. He radiated confidence and importance, and she felt drawn to him in the strangest way. It was almost as if she felt herself trusting him already. His features, while sharp and intimidating, made her feel safe. He was a little older, maybe in his early forties. He had deep frown lines that gave away his age, but his eyes were something else.

Claire was no stranger to interesting eyes. Her own were violet, and people always said how amazing they were. This man, though, had silver eyes that glowed. He stared at her intently, as if he were sizing her up. She felt like a wave of... something wash over her. It took her breath away, in the most literal sense. As abruptly as it began, the feeling dissipated. The glow of his eyes seemed to lessen, which caused Claire to wonder if she was seeing things.

"Claire, is it? My name is Vincent, and I was wondering if I could speak to you for a moment," he said.

She paused, then blurted, "And why would I do that?"

His lips kicked up in a slight smile. "Do you want to live here forever?"

As a matter of fact, she didn't want to live there forever. Who would? She let out a small grunt. "Touché."

His smile widened as he turned towards a room off the main entrance, reserved for potential parents. She still wasn't sure that following him was a good idea, but something about him just felt familiar. Should she trust her instincts? She figured she didn't have anything to lose. If she stayed here another two or three years she'd end up on the street, anyway. Might as well see what a stranger with oddly glowing eyes wanted.

This room was one she'd never seen before. In all the time she'd been at the orphanage, no one had ever tried to adopt her. It was simple, white like everything else, with two chairs opposite a desk. Much to Claire's surprise, Vincent turned a charming smile on Mary, who now stood transfixed by his gaze.

"Would you mind giving us a moment?" he asked.

Mary's returning smile was plastic and out of place. It sent a shiver down Claire's spine. "Of course," she said pleasantly before flouncing out of the room. Yes, flouncing.

Mary? Pleasant? Claire thought she'd never see the day. She eyed Vincent carefully, wondering if he would do something like that to her. She sure as shit hoped not.

"Have you noticed anything odd lately? Had any weird dreams?" he asked, that charming smile never slipping from his face.

Claire's spine stiffened. Yes, she had been having weird dreams, though they weren't exactly new. Was she going to tell an elite stranger that? Hell no. Elites weren't people that orphans could trust. Especially not ones with the power to mesmerize irritable madames. Then again, maybe she could talk this guy into doing something about Beth. If he turned out to be friendly, of course.

"I have no idea what you're talking about," Claire said, voicing lacking conviction. She was curious to see what the stranger would do. She did want to leave the orphanage, but she didn't want to end up dead, either.

Vincent's head tilted to the side. "If that is your final answer, I shall leave you."

With that, he strode towards the door.

Claire should let him go. She really should, but something in her was telling her to stop him. "Wait," she said, only a moment before he pressed the button that would slide the door open.

That charming smile was back in place. "Odd dreams, yes?" he asked in an amicable way.

Claire still wasn't certain that this was her best idea, but she went with it, anyway. "How do you know about that?"

"It's my job to know. What were your dreams about?"

Claire sighed, rubbing her sweaty palms over her plain, black pants. "It was…" she trailed off, unsure how to describe it, and then the words started tumbling out of her. "It was this beautiful place, unlike anything I've ever seen. It had trees and this… this… lagoon. It was amazing." She clamped her mouth shut, horrified that she'd admitted that to him. She hadn't meant to say all of that, and she had no idea why she had.

"Do you trust me?" Vincent asked.

She figured she might as well continue being honest. "Enough to think that you probably won't immediately murder me?" she shrugged. "Yeah, I guess." Completely sure he wouldn't? Not really. But reasonably.

"Then it's time for us to leave. We can't talk here."

Her mouth dropped open. Leave? She couldn't just leave. Didn't he have paperwork to fill out?

"I can't go anywhere with you," she argued. The guy wouldn't murder her here, but in an alley? What would stop him?

"But you can. It's been taken care of. Do you have any belongings you'd like to retrieve?"

"N-no," she stammered. Other than standard issue clothes, but even those weren't really hers. They were traded out on laundry day.

"Very well. Off we go." Without another word, Vincent exited the room. Claire followed close behind him and watched as he took a pile of papers from the madame's hand.

"Well, where are we going?" Claire asked.

"First, we're going to Redwater—"

"*Redwater*?" she interrupted. "But that's all the way across the country."

"Afraid of stepping outside of your comfort zone? I expected better from you, Claire."

"You shouldn't expect anything from me. You don't even know me."

"Touché," he said with a sly grin, echoing her words from before. Though he'd verbally conceded the point, she thought that he might know what to expect from her, anyway. Somehow.

Claire took one final look around the orphanage and decided that she'd miss nothing from here; it wasn't a home for her. She had no loyalty to the place, no friends here, and certainly no family. Leaving, even if it was with this strange man named Vincent, caused her to be secretly overjoyed. She suspected he was taking her home. After he filled out the paperwork to relieve Madame Mary of her "parental" duties, she followed him outside.

EVERTON WAS THE CAPITAL of the forest-ridden country of Easthaven, but you'd never know it from the industrial city that stood before her. The buildings around the orphanage were maybe four stories tall, completely stunted compared to the rest of the city. Most buildings rose to up to 400 stories and were made of steel, adorned with platinum decorations. There were maybe ten feet between each of the structures. The air was heavy with pollution, and at night, the city was a sea of lights. On every other block, statues of the current Minister stood to remind the people of their gracious leader. Claire had always found the obsession with the Minister a little cult-like.

Everton was a city of adoring, wealthy citizens. Crime was low, only existing around the orphanages and slums, and morale was always high. Lack of confidence in the Minister was minuscule, something that Claire found very odd given their democratic system of government, and he was widely admired by most of the citizens.

Vincent led her to the hover monorail station and purchased two tickets to Redwater. The monorails stood high off the ground, weaving through the city and beyond in intricate patterns. Claire felt sorry for the person who had to design this system but commended his genius. The monorail split at the edges of Everton to venture out to all of the major cities.

Redwater was rural compared to the grandiose scene of Everton. Claire had only heard rumors of the town, but it was the West-most city in the country, causing her to be confused as to why they would be going that far.

"So, are you going to tell me why we're going to Redwater?" Claire asked.

"Redwater isn't our final destination, we're going beyond it," Vincent said mysteriously.

"There's literally just trees beyond Redwater. You're taking me to the trees?" They couldn't go into a neighboring country. Claire didn't have the proper documentation.

His grin was wicked. "Clever girl."

"That tells me nothing," she said, a scoff escaping with the words.

"Yes, but more accurately, I'm taking you to the woods beyond there. You should know that." It was Vincent's turn to chuckle at his own words.

Claire furrowed her brow. "You mean the woods I've been seeing in my dreams?"

"'Dream' isn't the right word for it. Visions, if you will."

"You've got to be kidding me. I was adopted by a crazy person. Great. Perfect. Can we turn this thing around?" She asked rhetorically.

"You're not the only person experiencing these newfound…

abilities."

An odd sense of relief washed over her. The idea itself was insane. Abilities? What kind of bullshit was that? Sure, there were tall tales of people who had special abilities floating around Everton. Did Claire believe an ounce of those tales? Of course not. They were tales that parents told children to give them a fright before bed.

"They're not exactly new," she grumbled. If he was going to be all-knowing, he should at least know that.

"Stronger, then."

"So you've gone around Easthaven, just snatching up orphans and telling them they have visions?"

"Not only visions. Just before you I found a boy who is a beast master. He doesn't even know it yet. Be thankful I'm telling you what you can do. Though, most of the people you meet will be quite older than you. So, no, I'm not just snatching up orphans."

"Well, I'm certainly glad you don't discriminate."

"Of course not, that would make things very boring." Vincent gave her a warm smile, trying to reassure her that he wasn't totally insane. He was trying to show her that she would never regret the decision she made this day. Not that she had one. The pull to this wood couldn't be denied.

"Oh gods…" she muttered under her breath.

"Don't worry, I think you'll quite like where we're going."

Claire stared out of the window of the monorail. The instant they crossed out of Everton, the landscape changed drastically. That green color she'd seen in her dreams spanned as far as she could see. She couldn't help but press her hands against the window, her jaw dropping. Soon enough, they were immersed in a deep forest.

The bark of the forest wasn't nearly as dark as those in her dreams. This signaled to Claire that they were nowhere near their destination. Since she (mostly) trusted Vincent, she'd figured as much already.

The scene in front of her was so calming that she fell asleep for the rest of the ride. Vincent didn't mind this, he'd had enough of entertaining children for a lifetime.

Eventually, they arrived in Redwater. The station here was vastly different from the one they started with. There were no walls surrounding the station, and Claire felt like she could see the entirety of the town from that very spot. The station in Everton was probably the size of the entire city here. There was a simple, small teller's booth, and an awning covering the landing platform.

"This is... different," she mumbled.

"Not everywhere in the world is as conventionally beautiful as Everton," Vincent replied coolly.

Redwater was unlike anything Claire had ever seen. It was so much smaller than Everton, and the sophisticated monorail didn't look like it belonged. All around her were buildings with wooden frames filled with plaster. They had slightly curved roofs and pane glass windows. The streets were made of cobblestone, something Claire had never thought she'd see in person.

"How long are we staying here?" She asked.

Vincent cast her a glance over his shoulder. "Only the night."

Claire felt a tinge of disappointment. She didn't want to leave yet. She wanted to explore. Then again, she really wanted to see that place from her dreams.

Vincent took Claire to a small restaurant in the center of town. To her surprise, the food was actually good. She'd expected everything outside of Everton to be... well... less than, if you will. Instead, she found herself enjoying the clear air and the view of the clouds as the suns set. When the suns finally disappeared over the horizon, the breath left her lungs. The sky. She'd never seen the sky look like this. It was so magnificent. Instead of being a dull black with only a few stars, it lit up the town around her with more stars than she'd ever be able to count. She could actually see all of the cosmic phenomenon she'd only ever heard about. The constellations, clusters of stars, and brightly lit star dust, all of it was visible. Claire could have stared at it all night, but Vincent finally ushered her into the inn.

"Does the sky always look like that?" She couldn't help but ask, amazement clear in her tone.

A smile spread over Vincent's face. He hadn't been sure how Claire would handle this, but now he was confident that she would be okay. "Out here it does."

With that, Claire knew she never wanted to go back to Everton. Everything out here was just better. There was nature, the people were nicer, and you couldn't beat a sky like that. Even if Vincent was planning on ditching her, she knew she'd find a way to stay here.

THE NEXT MORNING, Vincent led her through the town until they came to a bridge that arched over a slowly moving river. As they crossed it, Claire saw that it led into woods with bark dark as pitch. The leaves, however, were every shade of green imaginable. There were deeply colored vines that snaked over the tree trunks. The canopies were lighter, the color rich under the morning suns.

As they entered the woods, Claire started recognizing the smells and sounds. The air smelled fresh and there was the rustle of animals all around her. The further they ventured, the more at home Claire began to feel. They were edging closer and closer to the land of her visions. Much to Claire's surprise, they still weren't there by midday. She finally decided to ask about it.

"How long until we get there?"

"Oh, only a few more hours. We should make it right at sundown."

Sundown? Oh no. This place had better be as amazing as her dreams promised.   As the suns were starting to set, Claire began to wonder if her legs would give out. Her muscles were beat, and her feet were sore. That, however, faded from her mind the moment she felt the boundary of the coven. The boundary wasn't visible, but the energy was palpable, causing her to stumble. There was a wave of sorts that ran down her body and out through her toes, causing the ground to tremble. Without warning, her eyes started to sting, and her hands flew up to clutch them.

"Son of a bitch," she hissed, sweat coating her skin.

Once the pain subsided, she glanced at Vincent, a question in her eyes.

"That's normal," he said nonchalantly, and they kept walking.

The trees seemed to thicken as they walked until she couldn't help but brush against them. She expected the bark to at least scratch her, the tunic she was wearing wasn't thick, but it didn't.

Vincent suddenly stopped at the edge of a clearing. Claire couldn't stop the tears from welling in her eyes at the scene. Home. That was the word that echoed through her head.

The trees were exquisite in detail, and Claire couldn't help but silently curse her visions for not doing this place justice. The trees felt as tall as the buildings in Everton, but instead of making her feel small, she felt endless power. The setting suns shone through the trees, giving an ethereal light to the scene in front of her.

There were fourteen round cabins arranged in a circle. They were all one-story homes with plenty of space in between each. They were all connected by a wooden planked courtyard, completing the circle. As Claire moved closer, she saw in the center of this circle a single, also circular, great table with a solid bench around the entirety of it. Pathways made of wooden planks from the doors of each cabin led to this point. A massive energy came from this table, the importance of it radiated throughout the clearing. She could tell this was the source of some great power.

Claire moved closer to the table and laid one hand down to feel the organic structure. She expected it to be rough like the exterior of the trees, but the smoothness surprised her. While the table appeared to be handcrafted, it was still too perfect.

She started to glance around at the houses surrounding her. They were all perfectly matching on the exterior, with French wooden doors with small windows. The other windows had curtains drawn over them, giving her no insight for what, or who, was living on the inside. She started walking around the table, looking at each individual house. She stopped in front of one, staring at it intently. The curtains were drawn just enough for her to see a piano in the front of the room. This one felt like home. She continued walking before stopping in front of another one. She couldn't see inside of it, but a strange energy radiated from it. This one felt like forever.

"Welcome to the Blackwoods Coven," Vincent said.

TWO

"I GET TO STAY HERE?" she asked, her eyes wide with wonder.

Vincent smiled warmly. "This your new home."

His words weren't empty, that she knew. The surrounding woods had felt like home for years now, even if it was only in her dreams. She almost felt like hugging Vincent, oddly enough, but resisted the urge.

Looking around at the cabins, she wondered which one she would stay in. As it turned out, she didn't have to wonder for long. Vincent led her to a cabin on the right side of the courtyard. This was the first of the two that she'd stopped in front of only moments ago. Her heart started to hammer in her chest as she wondered what it would be like inside. Until yesterday, she'd only seen buildings in Everton, and this was a far cry from Everton. Most life-time residents never saw trees, woods, or natural running water. Claire still couldn't believe that she was really here.

Before they reached the cabin, a cheerful looking woman approached. She was abnormally tall, like Vincent. Claire was quite tall herself, but this woman had a few inches on her. She had a kind face with bright green eyes that held a glow similar to Vincent's.

Claire wondered if everyone here would have eyes like that. Her platinum blonde hair was up in an intricate series of braids that showed off her full lips and sharp features that weren't typical for people of Easthaven. She was absolutely beautiful, possibly the most beautiful woman Claire had ever seen. Claire guessed that she was at least fifteen years older than her, if not more.

"Care to introduce us?" the woman asked in a melodic tone. She had an accent that Claire had never heard before. Her smile only amplified her perfectly formed features.

"Of course," Vincent said, matching her smile. "Farrah, this Claire. Claire, Farrah."

"It's wonderful to meet you, Claire," Farrah said, turning that infectious smile her way. Her voice felt like a warm hug.

Claire couldn't help but smile back. "It's nice to meet you, too."

"Would you mind if I showed her to her room?" Farrah asked Vincent.

"Of course. I'll see you both in the morning." With that, Vincent strode towards the center of the courtyard. Claire furrowed her brow. She couldn't quite make out what happened next since it was nighttime, but there was a loud sound, and she saw something shift before Vincent disappeared into the floor.

"He lives underground," Farrah said helpfully. Claire supposed that kind of explained what had just happened, but she still didn't understand the mechanics behind it.

Once they got to the round cabin that would be Claire's, Farrah simply waved her hand, and the double doors swung open.

Claire's eyes widened with shock. "How did you…"

Farrah turned back to her, a wide grin on her face. "Magic, darling. You'll learn everything in time. Come see your home."

Slowly, Claire entered the cabin. It smelled strongly of woods and something light and fresh. The walls and floors were all made of wood, as were the counters and cabinets. To her left was a seating area with comfortable looking couches and furniture. To her right was a full kitchen. In the center, of all things, was a grand piano.

"This is all mine?" Claire asked, shifting her gaze to Farrah.

"Half of it is. You'll have a roommate. Her name is Blayne."

Claire's stomach dropped. It wasn't that she was opposed to living with someone - because she wasn't - she was just scared that her roommate wouldn't like her. She almost laughed at herself. Never in her life had she been worried about what someone thought of her, yet here she was.

Farrah put her hand on Claire's arm, as if sensing her unease. "Don't worry. I think you and Blayne will get along just fine."

Claire gave her a grateful smile. "Where is she?"

"She's probably with some of the other coven members. She'll be back soon. Would you like to see your room?"

Claire nodded, and Farrah started for the door on the back left side of the cabin. With another wave of her hand, the bedroom door slid open into the wall. The room was large and wooden like everything else with a nice looking bed in the center.

"On the right you'll find your washroom, and the dressers are fully stocked with the clothes that we wear. You can decorate however you like."

Claire frowned. "Will the clothes fit me?" she asked, skepticism coloring her voice. She couldn't imagine how they would have gathered enough clothes of her exact size on such short notice.

Farrah's smile was patient and understanding. "You'll find that they'll fit you quite well." Claire just stared at her, not quite believing what she was saying. "Vincent knew you were coming," Farrah added with a wink. "There are many things we'll be explaining to you in the morning, but you should catch on quick."

Claire was still struggling to comprehend everything. Since her parents died, she'd hadn't had anything that was truly hers. Sure, she didn't purchase anything here, but personal space was something she could appreciate. Yeah, she'd had to share the common area, but her own washroom? Privacy? That was a foreign concept from the orphanage she came from.

"Are you from Everton, too?" she asked, suddenly curious.

"No. I'm from Portsmouth."

Claire gaped at her. "Portsmouth? As in Paralia?" Paralia was halfway across the world. Getting from Portsmouth to here would be quite the feat. That explained her sharp features and accent.

"Yes, I'm quite a long way from home. It's worth it, though. Have trust," Farrah said.

Farrah explained a few things about coven life. Apparently, each member of the coven was expected to eat breakfast and dinner at the wooden table in the center of the courtyard, and each member was encouraged to become friends with everyone. The covens relied on camaraderie to stay strong. Once the coven reached full capacity, there would be twenty-nine of them: fourteen men and fourteen women, all under Vincent's leadership. As of Claire's arrival, there were twelve members. Claire still didn't know exactly what being in a coven really meant or what her life would be like.

There was one rule that shocked Claire the most. She knew a catch was coming; that this place wasn't going to be just a haven. Farrah explained that once the coven reached its full capacity, people could still arrive to claim their place in their new home. When this would happen, someone of the same sex would have to die. As Farrah said it, her gentle and calm demeanor never slipped. Somehow, Claire knew it wasn't an act. At the same time, she knew that despite how disturbed she was and how hard her heart was beating, there was something else running through her veins. Something along the wood and in the air. Something in this place—in this boundary— that was telling her it was the right thing, even if she didn't want to believe it. Even if, at the moment, she couldn't believe it.

"I know it's a lot to take in," Farrah whispered, looking as distressed as Claire felt. Telling the new members about this wasn't easy. There just wasn't a good way to break the news. Hell, Farrah herself could hardly believe what she was saying. There was just something in the magic of the coven itself that promised it would be okay. That this was the right thing.

Claire gave her a wry smile. "That's an understatement."

Just a little while later, the front doors of the cabin opened, and a very tall girl with light brown hair and glowing greenish-brown eyes stepped inside. When she saw Farrah and Claire standing in the kitchen, she paused and gave them an irritated look.

"What's going on?" she asked, her attention directed towards Farrah.

"Blayne, this is Claire. She's your new roommate. Play nice, please, she's still a bit unnerved," Farrah replied, her radiant smile never fading from her face.

Blayne seemed to study Claire, as if sizing her up. Normally, Claire would have glared right back, but in that moment she felt nervous and out of place. When Blayne finally smiled, it transformed her features from combative to mildly pleasant. Still, there was something kind of... off about her. She was pretty enough, Claire supposed, a few years older than her. Blayne smelled like woods and fresh water.

"Sorry it took me so long to get back," Blayne said apologetically to Farrah. "I was with Dex."

"That's quite alright," Farrah said, slowly walking to the front door. "I will leave you two to get settled in. See you in the morning."

Claire had the irrational urge to beg Farrah to stay, but of course she didn't. If she was going to make this work, she'd have to make nice with Blayne and not make a fool of herself by begging someone she barely knew to hold her hand.

"Are you from Easthaven?" Claire asked after the doors closed behind Farrah. She knew it was kind of lame, but she didn't know what else to ask.

Blayne pinned her with a dubious look. "I'm from Redwater. You?"

"Everton."

Blayne lifted an eyebrow. "Have you met anyone else yet?" she asked.

Claire shrugged. "Just you, Farrah, and Vincent."

The pinched look never left Blayne's face. "I think you'll fit in."

"Thanks," she said. There was a lull in conversation, leaving Claire to glance around and suddenly point to the piano. "I haven't seen one of these in person before. You play?" She asked.

"Nah," Blayne said casually, "it came with the place when I got here."

"Oh...cool! Guess I can learn now..." Claire drifted off.

Blayne sighed. "I've been running around for a few hours now, though, so I'm going to take a shower before my stink reaches you then head to bed. If you need anything, give me a knock. If you're hungry, there're some snacks in the kitchen."

Claire was a little thrown off by her briskness. "Okay, see you in the morning."

Claire walked around the kitchen, opening cabinets as she moved. She opened the ice box to see mostly vegetables, which she gladly ate.

Once she was full, she retreated to her new room. She went into the washroom first and stopped very suddenly in front of the mirror. She moved closer and stared at her eyes. As she looked closely at them, her heart rate picked up and her breathing became ragged. There was no way this was happening. Things like this just didn't happen. They had developed that same glow that Vincent, Farrah, and Blayne had. Her before flat, purple eyes were now effervescent. She couldn't help but gape. She really liked how they looked, but she was also scared. Her eye color was very rare, and it had always made her stand out. She'd hoped that living with people who had glowing eyes would take the attention away from her, but now she was thinking that she wouldn't be so lucky.

The exhaustion from her journey over the past thirty-six hours set in. She sighed and decided to take a shower before crawling into bed.

After showering, she went to the dresser in her bedroom. All of the clothes in there were fairly plain, but she settled with loose-fitting grey pants and a long sleeved black shirt. She was asleep before her head hit the pillow.

CLAIRE WOKE AFTER THE BEST NIGHT'S SLEEP she'd had in a very long time. She couldn't remember the last time she hadn't had a vision in her sleep. The air here was nothing like it was in Everton. Just like in her visions, it was crisp and clean, even inside the cabins. She ventured into the living room where Blayne was already waiting for her.

"Well, it's about time," Blayne said with a wry smile. "You almost missed breakfast."

Claire searched for a clock on the wall, but she didn't see one. "How do you know what time it is?" she asked.

"You'll get the hang of it. Let's go."

She'd get the hang of it? What did that even mean?

They left the cabin and stepped onto the wooden-planked courtyard. The morning air was cool, and it was inexplicably bright despite all the tree cover. Claire took a deep breath, still not over how great the air made her feel. She could sense the life coursing through the ground surrounding her, something she'd never sensed before. She wondered if this was another part of being in a coven. Then again, it could also be that she was just actually surrounded by trees.

It was then that Claire wondered where any of the food came from. She hadn't seen any gardens or livestock.

"Blayne?" she asked.

"Yeah?"

"Where do we get food?"

Blayne laughed. "It's just another one of those things. Who knows why the coven magic does anything or where any of this magic comes from."

Claire wasn't satisfied with that answer, but she was pretty sure Blayne wasn't satisfied with it, either. Claire was familiar with most of the major religions. The most prominent one in Easthaven was polytheistic, but there were some others. There was a monotheistic religion mostly contained to the country of Azmar, but that was on another continent. Another country, Solaris, was known for its cosmic-like beliefs. They believed in a greater power that held the magic of the world together—the magic that powered all of their technology. Claire didn't know what to believe. Every society had stories about magical beings, but she'd bet none of them had gotten it quite right.

Her eyes locked onto one of the people sitting at the table. A boy about her age sat directly across from where she was standing. Her heart shot up into her throat, and her breath caught as his ocean blue eyes met hers. The morning suns reflected off his dark brown hair, giving it golden highlights. He had full lips, arched cheekbones, and a stern brow. He was stunning. Claire was almost in a trance, memorizing every detail in his face. Somehow, she knew it was one she'd never want to forget.

She was in awe, most of all, of his iridescent eyes. She could have sworn that she'd seen this color before, and a feeling of belonging came over her. The way that he looked at her made her think that maybe he was in this same trance, as his eyes didn't shift from hers for even a moment.

Her trance was suddenly broken when Blayne said, "Claire? Hello? Where do you want to sit?"

Claire snapped her eyes away, a blush coloring her cheeks. "Uh… wherever you want," she stammered. Her gaze immediately shot back to him, to find that he was still looking at her. This time, though, he had a smirk on his face. That smirk only caused her blush to deepen and her heart to trip up in her chest.

Blayne led them to the opposite side of the large table.

"Who's that?" Claire asked, tilting her head towards the boy. She was trying to be sly, but she could tell by his growing grin that she wasn't doing a very good job.

Blayne rolled her eyes at Claire as she sat down. "Dex, and you don't need to worry about him. He's happily taken."

Claire blinked, taken aback by Blayne's demeanor. "Oh. Okay, makes sense. I guess." Then she remembered the name of the boy Blayne had been with last night. Claire wondered if Blayne meant he was taken by her. She quietly took her seat next to Blayne, daring another glance at Dex. When she saw that he was also glancing at her, she couldn't help the smile that tipped the corners of her mouth.

Farrah set next to Claire, drawing her attention away from Dex. "Good morning, Claire. Did you sleep well?" she asked with a friendly smile.

Claire smiled back at her. "Yes, I did."

Without thinking, Claire's eyes went back to Dex. One or two glances were okay, but this was getting ridiculous. When she looked back, Farrah was glancing between the two with a small smile.

Claire pointedly ignored that and started eating, making small talk throughout breakfast until Farrah spoke with a serious, yet sincere tone.

"Blayne, why don't you give me some time with Claire? I want to get to know her a little better."

Blayne gave Farrah a look that said, "What are you really up to?" but she didn't ask out loud. Instead, she stood and went back to the cabin. Claire was getting the sense that there was another unofficial leader in this coven. Farrah gestured for the two of them to stand and walked a little bit away from the table. Now that Blayne was gone, she took another look at Dex.

When Dex stood, Claire saw that he was tall. Not as tall as Vincent, but Claire would have to crane her neck to look at him. He was lean, but she could see faint traces of muscle underneath his navy blue wrap. His pants were molded to his long legs, and Claire couldn't help but look him up and down as he walked passed her. Farrah didn't even try to hide her devilish grin. When she saw that Farrah was following after Dex, her heart started to pound in her chest.

"Dex," Farrah called.

Uh oh, Claire thought.

He turned, his blue eyes landing on Farrah. The smile on his face made Claire's heart stop. He was gorgeous, anyway, but when he smiled he was almost unbelievable.

"Have you met the newest member of our coven?" she asked.

His eyes drifted over Claire before returning to meet her gaze. She felt like she couldn't breathe. There was something about him that she couldn't name.

"As a matter of fact, I haven't," he said.

Claire already found herself wanting to roll her eyes at him. "Hi. It's Dex, right?"

He held out his hand, confidence radiating from him. "Nice to meet you, Claire. Vincent told us he was bringing someone new, but he didn't tell us it'd be someone like you." Dex's eyes ran up and down her body, deepening her blush. She shook his hand, feeling electricity as they touched.

"Oh-uh-well, I didn't know that everyone knew that I was coming," she stammered. She sounded like a love-struck teenager, stumbling over her words and making no sense. In hindsight, it made her a little sick at herself, even if it was kind of true.

He smirked at her. "Even if we didn't, I noticed you right away."

She didn't think that her face could feel more hot after he said that. "I - uh…"

Farrah let out a small gasp. "Well, I guess I did my job. You kids have fun," she smiled warmly as she walked away. It was then that Claire realized the full extent of what Farrah had done.

Before Claire could be shocked by that Dex asked, "So, where did Vincent find you?"

"Everton," she said softly. She didn't want him to know she was from an orphanage. No matter where he was from, that wasn't something to brag about. Besides, Claire wasn't a fan of pitying looks, and she knew dead parents was a surefire way to get them.

His smile widened. "Me too! What part of Everton are you from?"

She felt her heart drop. "The seventh sector," she said. It wasn't technically a lie. That was where she lived before her parents died.

"No way. You've got to be kidding me. I'm from the sixth. It's insane that we never ran into each other."

She let out a small chuckle. "Yeah, totally insane. I was mostly a homebody. My parents had me homeschooled."

"Well that's why. I used to hang out with tons of kids from seventh. I'm pretty sure my parents and brothers moved there, now that I'm gone." He seemed a little... bitter, almost, at them. The seventh sector was much nicer than the sixth, so it made sense for them to move up in the world with one less mouth to feed. Also, siblings weren't a common phenomenon in Everton. It was rare for couples to have children in general, let alone more than one.

"Brothers? What's that like?" Claire asked.

"They're amazing. Little shits, honestly, but I love them. They're twins, Greg and Jorgen. They're six right now," he said with a sad smile. It was obvious that these boys meant the world to Dex, and being without them tore him up.

"That must be wonderful. I'm sure having siblings is great."

They wanted the conversation to continue, but Vincent cleared his throat. He stood on the table in the center of the complex, drawing Claire's attention away from the very handsome boy in front of her. His voice was naturally amplified as he said, "Everyone, we have a new member, as you may have seen. I'm going to re-explain guard duty for her benefit."

Everyone turned to stare at Vincent, as if drawn by magnets. Even his eyes seemed to shine brighter. Members who had already returned to their cabins emerged, transfixed on their leader.

"As most of you know, two members have guard duty each night and they scout the perimeter for any potential threats or trespassers. Sam. May. Tonight is your night. Your shift begins when the suns go down."

A tall, redheaded woman with a light, rosy complexion and an even taller man with smooth, dark skin looked at each other and nodded with friendly smiles. Claire couldn't help but smile at the sight of them. Despite Blayne's frosty demeanor, everyone else seemed nice and like they really seemed to trust one another.

That made Claire think back to the rules of the coven. What if May and Sam lost each other? What would that do to them? She didn't know the exact nature of their relationship, but they seemed close.

Vincent stepped off the table with an inhuman grace before approaching Claire and Dex.

"Mind if I steal her from you?" he asked.

Dex gave Claire another long look before he shifted his attention back to Vincent. His look said that he did indeed mind, but of course he wasn't about to vocalize that opinion.

"Of course not," he said smoothly before striding away. Before he was even halfway across the courtyard, Blayne trotted up to him and linked her arm through his. Claire couldn't help the pang that sliced through her chest, nor could she explain it.

Belatedly, Claire realized she was staring and quickly snapped her eyes away, giving Vincent her undivided attention. It seemed that her longing look wasn't lost on him. His sly, sardonic smile proved that. Even so, he did her the courtesy of not mentioning it.

"You will need to be taught magic. You have it within you of course, that is why you are here, but formal training is required."

"I've never done anything magical," Claire said slowly. "Only the visions."

Vincent's smile widened. "Once you are inside the coven boundary, your powers are awakened. You've noticed the change in your eyes, have you not?"

"Well, yeah, of course I did." She'd also been quite shocked, though now she figured it made sense given that everyone else had glowing eyes, and she remembered the stinging sensation at the boundary.

"Would you be comfortable with Farrah showing you the ropes?"

Would she ever. Sure, she'd only met Farrah last night, but she already loved being around her. Claire understood why Farrah had been the one to tell her about the rules. She just had this motherly way about her.

"Well, I'm very glad to hear that," Farrah's charming voice said from behind her.

Vincent nodded with a slight bow. "I'll leave you to it, then."

Claire turned to Farrah, a smile on her lips. "So, how do we do this?"

"Well, it's not complicated. We'll start with elemental magic. How about fire?"

Claire nodded. She supposed that was as good a place to start as any.

"Excellent. Just hold your hand out and—" Suddenly, there was a flame flickering above Farrah's palm. Claire was standing close enough to feel the heat radiating from it. Then she closed her hand, and the flame was gone. "You try," Farrah said with a smile.

"O-okay," Claire said. Tentatively, Claire turned up her own palm and tried to will fire to appear, but nothing happened. Her eyes flicked back to Farrah.

"Don't worry. You'll get there. Try again."

Again, Claire tried and again, it didn't work.

Rather than backing down, Claire decided she had to make this work. Suddenly, a large flame came from the palm of her hand. She gasped loudly and tried with everything in her power to not let it get out of control. Before she could embarrass herself, she closed her hand and the flame went out.

"You caught on fast!" Farrah said cheerfully. "Has anyone explained affinities to you, though?"

Claire shook her head quickly, still reeling from what she just accomplished. "I'm assuming it's something I'm good at."

Farrah gave a sweet laugh. "Clear your mind and just focus in on what's inside of you, it'll come naturally."

Claire stood and closed her eyes, taking a deep breath. It took a few moments, but she finally focused on the magical energy inside of her, thinking about her visions. She felt the rocks and the trees more than anything. The ground beneath her felt like it was starting to quake and reach out to her. Suddenly, her hands were in fists and covered in various rocks that shot up from the ground surrounding them. One by one, they kept flying and attaching themselves to her. Her arms, parts of her shoulders, and up to her knees were completely covered in rocks before they stopped running to her. She was overwhelmed with excitement and was breathing heavily. She ignored the lightheadedness she was feeling; this was a high for her. She didn't think she'd ever amount to anything more than spending the rest of her days being miserable and knowing this power was inside of her the entire time brought her a new life. Claire finally opened her eyes, and all the rocks tumbled to the ground around her.

Dex smiled and let out a deep chuckle. "Well, what do you know? New girl's got game."

Claire jumped, surprised that he was behind her.

Blayne arched an eyebrow, "Seems so."

Farrah had a wide smile on her face. "Earth it is, then."

"Let me at her," Dex said, taking a step towards her. He took a deep breath and soon had rocks hovering around him.

"What do you plan on doing?" Claire asked, her eyes going wide.

"Break them," he said, laughing. Instantaneously, a rock started flying towards Claire, and as if a new instinct broke out inside of her, she shattered it before it got too close. One by one, he threw them over with his mind, and she destroyed them. They both had wide smiles on their faces when he was finished.

"That was incredible," Claire breathed.

"Yeah, so, we all can manipulate the four elements: air, fire, water, and earth. Some people, though, are just cool enough to be mostly connected with the earth." Dex approached her and raised his hand up for a high five, which she completed.

They didn't notice Vincent standing next to Farrah until this moment. He started slowly clapping his hands with a wide smile.

"Nothing makes me happier than seeing my new members come into their own. You two seem to work well together, so you'll be on guard duty together from now on. I'll announce when during breakfast the day of."

Claire was overjoyed to spend more time with Dex. The connection she felt with him had to continue—it had to grow. She wanted it more than anything.

THREE

OVER THE NEXT WEEK, Claire was buzzing with nervous anticipation of being on guard duty with Dex. First of all, guard duty felt like a lot of responsibility. Secondly, she would be on guard duty with Dex. No other newcomers had arrived in her short time at the coven, but she'd been assured that would change. Vincent would either take more trips into the outside world, or some people would just be drawn to the coven themselves. She supposed she'd been one of those people; the ones drawn to this place. How else do you explain those visions?

Claire wondered how long it would take for them to reach capacity and how long after that when the thirtieth person would arrive. Speaking of the outside world, she was pleased to know that they weren't confined to the coven boundaries. They were allowed to leave. Redwater was where most members went if they wanted new clothes or something to decorate their rooms. Claire hoped she'd get a chance to do that soon. The younger members like her were expected to be escorted by an adult, but she didn't mind that. Knowing she wouldn't be confined to the coven made her feel less claustrophobic.

As she got ready, she found herself nervously fidgeting with her

27

hair. If she wore it up, it showed off her high cheekbones and bright violet eyes. On the other hand, she wouldn't be able to push her hair in front of her face if he made her blush. And let's face it, Dex would absolutely make her blush. On the other *other* hand, it would be dark out. He wouldn't be able to see her blush.

But... they did have enhanced night vision. Yeah, it was official. Claire was a lost cause. In the end, she went with clipping the front of her hair back. That way, it was out of her face, but her nice, natural waves were still visible. She groaned as she stared at herself in the mirror. She would never get this right, and she was out of time. She did her best to make sure that her fitted black outfit wasn't dirty. It wasn't, as far as she could tell, and even if it was, she had to go. Blayne had been correct about developing that internal clock. There was no time to keep fussing in the mirror.

She took a deep breath, trying to steady herself and went to leave the cabin. To her surprise, Blayne wasn't in the living room. At this hour, she usually was. She frowned, but didn't waste time trying to find her. Instead, she stepped out into the cool night air. The coven smelled good during the day, but it was even better when the suns went down. Everything was so fresh and open out here. Claire didn't know if she'd ever get used to it.

She spotted Dex right away. He was sitting casually at the main table, dressed in the standard guard uniform. Right next to him was Blayne.

Her step faltered as she approached, suddenly unsure of what to say. Blayne gave her a once-over before a plastic smile appeared.

"Love the outfit," she said with a wink.

What the hell did that mean? Had they been close, Claire would have assumed that it was a cheeky nod to the fact that they didn't choose the outfits, but since they weren't, she couldn't be sure.

"Thanks?" she almost asked.

Blayne stood fluidly, giving Claire a hearty whiff of her perfume. Had there been less of it, it would have smelled good.

Her laugh was light and airy. "Relax. It's a compliment." She passed Claire before tossing Dex a heated look over her shoulder. "See you later," she purred.

When Claire dared a glance at Dex, she was startled to find him looking at her instead of Blayne. His bright blue eyes were fixed on her face, and that lazy smirk was doing very strange things to her heart.

"Hi," she said, getting a hold of herself. She even managed to smile at him. Assuming that it didn't make her like an idiot, but it probably did.

She guessed that it didn't because the dreamy look in his eyes didn't fade as he rose to his feet. "You ready?" he asked as he drew close enough for her to smell the cologne he was wearing. It smelled like an amplified version of the earth surrounding them. Considering his affinity, she wondered if it was cologne at all.

"As I'll ever be." With that, they started for the woods. Claire looked up at the sky, still in awe even though she'd been there for almost a week.

"It's cool, isn't it?" Dex asked, catching what she was staring at.

"It's unbelievable." She met his eyes with a genuine smile. Once they got to the tree line, she finally tore her gaze from the sky and watched where she was going. She still couldn't believe how well she could see in the dark. There weren't any lights out here, so she should have been completely blind. It wasn't crystal clear, but it was good enough to get by.

"So what do we actually do on guard duty?" she asked.

Dex gave her a wicked smile. "We're supposed to be on the look out for intruders. Not that I think that any can show up, or even enter the coven because of the barrier. They'd just walk right through the coven as if it's not there."

"That's weird. Then why do we have to do this?"

Dex shrugged. "I'm assuming it's just practice. Covens are very volatile and aren't full-fledged until they reach a thousand years old. Obviously, it's rare for a coven to make it."

Claire's eyebrows went up. "Wait, a thousand years? Does that mean Vincent won't be the leader forever? Who takes over?"

Dex shook his head. "If we're within the boundaries of a coven, we stop aging once our bodies are done developing."

"No one told me that. I'm not sure I want to live to a thousand years old," Claire muttered. Who would want to live that long? Maybe a few hundred years, sure. But one thousand? She supposed

Farrah left out that detail for a reason.

Dex chuckled, though she thought there was some darkness behind that laugh. "You'll have me around, so I can't imagine it'd be so bad."

Claire blushed. She couldn't imagine being in the body of a twenty-two-year-old forever, but the thought of having Dex around wasn't... so bad. Okay, maybe that was a little insane. She'd just met him, and she apparently had a thousand years ahead of her. Yeah. She needed to slow down.

"Did Farrah or Vincent explain what happens after we reach capacity?" Dex asked sheepishly.

Claire nodded, a knot forming in her throat. "Yeah. How do you feel about that?" She'd wanted to ask someone who'd been here longer to gauge their reaction.

He sighed. "It sucks, really, that eventually we will lose someone who is here. It makes sense, though. We need to get stronger if we'll make it to a thousand years, and that requires new people, new insight. There's a balance in the magic here, you can feel it already, and this just maintains that balance."

Claire focused on the air and trees surrounding her. He was right, there was a balance. Things were as they should be. She obviously struggled with this dark fact, but she also supposed that there was a reason for this. The magic wouldn't require it if it wouldn't give something just as good back to the coven.

"Have you found any cool spots?" she asked. Sure, they were supposed to be on the lookout for intruders. Should they be exploring? No, but Claire was curious. This place was too beautiful not to explore, and she wanted to find all of the places she'd seen in her visions for years.

That devilish grin was back on his face. "I've found a few things." His pace quickened so that Claire struggled to keep up. It felt like they were walking forever when they came across a massive tree. All the trees were tall, but they didn't look like this. This tree had an enormous trunk and rose higher than all the trees around it.

"Pretty sweet, right?" Dex said.

"Yeah," Claire replied, completely in awe. She felt her response was too simple, but that was all she could find herself saying.

"It gets better. Follow me."

Dex jogged up to the tree and took a deep breath. A column of solid rock lifted him up to the first solid branch of the tree. He grabbed onto it and sat down, glancing down at Claire. The column receded back into the ground.

"You coming?" he yelled.

Claire was confused for a second. She walked to the spot where he was just standing, closed her eyes, and focused her energy on the ground below her. She envisioned a column of rock lifting her into the air, wind rushing around her, flying past Dex, and stopping towards the top of the tree. When she opened her eyes, she was in between a bundle of branches. She looked around, trying to find Dex.

"Show off," Dex yelled, a wide smile on his face. Claire looked down and found him maybe fifteen feet below her. Show off indeed, she thought. He climbed branches the rest of the way up to her.

They were far above the other trees. The air seemed to be even clearer up here, and Claire took a deep breath. Pine filled the air, and she couldn't tell if she was smelling more of the trees or of Dex. She looked around to the surrounding area, seeing if she could get her bearings. To her right, she could see the coven with her enhanced vision. It was gorgeous, even from this far away. She could even make out some of the cabins from here.

Claire made her way to the other side of the tree trunk and looked out in front of her. Something… glowing… caught her eye in the distance. She couldn't really see what it was from up here, but she wanted to find out.

"Do you see that?" she asked, pointing towards the glow.

He shifted, trying to look over her shoulder. Finally he stilled, and she heard his intake of breath. "I've never seen that before," he almost whispered.

"Any idea what it is?" she asked, keeping her voice low. In retrospect, she didn't know why she did that, but she did it nonetheless.

He shook his head. "No idea. We have to go check it out." He summoned a column in front of them, and they both stepped onto it. The column wasn't wide enough for them to both stand comfortably, so they stood facing each other with maybe a few inches in between them. When the descent started, Claire instinctually grabbed onto Dex for support. Her heart was pounding out of her chest at his proximity, and she was suddenly aware of how loud she was breathing. Her face was hot, and he only looked down at her with a smirk when her hand landed on his arm. He placed his hand on her arm as well. All too soon, it was over, and they were back down on the ground. She held his ocean blue gaze for a heartbeat before backing away and dropping her hand. That would have been embarrassing, if not for the sheepish look on his face as well.

Claire nodded, and they started jogging towards that residual glow. They came upon a river, and they followed it to their destination. Claire wondered where it came from considering she couldn't see it from the tree. As they went, the river started to glow. They heard the roaring of a waterfall before they should see it.

Claire started to jog, eager to see what kind of waterfall could make that much noise. Dex had no issue keeping up with her pace and before long, they were at the edge of a massive cliff. She carefully stepped towards the edge, trying to see over it. He grabbed her arm, pulling her back slightly. She turned to look at him, and he gave her a weak smile.

"Just don't want you to fall off," he said.

She didn't want to fall off either, but she did want to see what was at the bottom of that cliff. She leaned over again, and her breath caught in her throat at the sight before her. The water was so unbelievably blue, and it was glowing in the moonlight. Suddenly, she realized where she'd seen the blue of Dex's eyes before. It was in her visions of this lagoon. She wanted nothing more than to get down there, but the cliff was a straight drop, and who knows how far it went down. She wasn't sure she could hold on to some kind of rock pillar that long.

"This is incredible," Dex breathed, leaning over next to Claire.

"You didn't know this was here?" she asked curiously.

"I had no idea."

"How do we get down there?" she asked, frustration coloring her tone.

"No clue," he muttered under his breath.

It wasn't long until guard duty was ending, and both of them felt it.

"I don't want to go back. This place is just gorgeous. Too bad there's no way to get down there without dying," Dex said.

"I don't think either one of us could maintain a pillar that large," she added.

He nodded in agreement. "I've only been here a little over a month, I don't have total control yet."

Another internal alert went through their bodies, signaling that it was time to return, the first of the two suns peaking over the horizon.

"We have to leave," Dex said.

"I know," she replied. Neither of them moved for another few moments, but then they both started to walk back without another word. The lagoon was all Claire could think about. It was the most beautiful thing she'd ever seen.

WHEN BREAKFAST CAME AROUND later that morning, Claire didn't even speak to Blayne as she left their cabin. She went straight to Dex, sitting down next to him at the table with her food.

"We gotta go back," she said, leaning close to him, keeping her voice low. Her lids were heavy. They still needed to sleep.

"You're right. We have to find a way down to that pool, too," Dex said.

"But how can we?"

Dex's eyes grew wide. "I have a rope ladder—well, most of us have them. The edge of the coven is full of cliffs. We can anchor it down with some rocks. It's crazy long, so we should be able to make it all the way down. If not, a platform should be well within our powers. We could go after breakfast."

"We need to sleep," Claire said, sounding exhausted.

Reluctantly, Dex agreed. "When we're done, meet me at the tree," he whispered. She knew exactly what he meant.

When Dex strode to his cabin, Blayne slid next to him and laid her hand on his bicep. Claire saw her say something, but she couldn't hear what was said. Dex grimaced and gestured towards Claire. Blayne glanced at her, her mouth forming into a tight line. Dex said something else, and Blayne crossed her arms. He ran a hand over his face, then seemed to apologize. Blayne's disgruntled expression softened, and her cheeks heated as she started swaying side to side, a happy grin on her face.

Finally, Blayne sauntered off, and Dex made it into his cabin with a shake of his head. He didn't know when he'd keep his promise to Blayne, but he would figure something out.

After a few hours of sleep, he rummaged around under his bed, and finally managed to wrestle out the folded up rope ladder. He coughed a little at the plume of dust that assaulted his nose before sneezing. How could that much dust accumulate in just a month? He shook out the ladder, keeping his head turned away. Once the dust cloud cleared, and he deemed the ladder good enough, he made his way towards their tree.

No one stopped him as he edged towards the tree line. They were allowed to do whatever they wanted during the day as long as they made it back for dinner. Still, he was grateful that no one had noticed him. He stumbled over a branch or two as he went. He saw the tree first, but his eyes were trained on Claire. Her hair was a gorgeous mixture of brown and deep violet, and it was even more brilliant in the suns. When she smiled at him, he couldn't help but smile back.

"Will that be long enough?" Claire asked, eyeing the bundle tucked under his arm. She hadn't doubted him when he'd told her, but now that she saw how small the folded up ladder was, she wasn't convinced.

He smirked. "We have some magic that lets us make really large things easier to store."

Claire folded her arms across her chest. He could have told her about that before. He was the one teaching her about magic for the most part, after all. But of course, he hadn't. She'd make sure to get him back. Later.

She wiped the cross look off her face and replaced it with a jaded smile. Dex caught that look, but he ignored it as she said, "Let's go!"

With that, they were off. Headed towards the cliff and to that lagoon Claire had seen so many times in her visions. Her heart started to pound when she neared the rushing water. Excitement bubbled up with every step they took along the river bank. Once they got there and looked down, they both stared in awe. The lagoon was amazing at night, but it was nothing compared to how it looked during the day. In the illuminating rays of the suns, they could see every minute detail. The glowing water poured over the rocks, the rocks glistening in the suns, and there was a rainbow created by the spray of the water splashing down from the waterfall.

Dex unfolded the ladder and sent it down the cliff, holding onto the top end of it. He placed the top rung under his foot and rocks emerged from the ground, wrapping themselves around the top rung like roots of a tree.

He tested it by pulling as hard as he could. "I think that's stable enough," he said excitedly.

Claire was almost jumping out of her skin. "I'll go first."

Dex gave her a pointed look that clearly said, "I'm the guy, this is a dangerous rope ladder above a cliff, so I should go first," but she ignored that and pushed him aside.

Claire climbed down the ladder. It was longer than the cliff itself, which was remarkable. When she set her feet on the ground, she immediately turned around to see the view in front of her.

She barely heard it when Dex hit the ground. She was too stunned by the scene. There was a crystal blue pool, and the roaring of the waterfall made a wave of calmness rain over her. She breathed in deeply to smell the mineral water, letting it wash over her. The waterfall came down in all different places, cascading over the rocks. Claire and Dex never wanted to leave this place. They stood next to each other, completely astounded by the scene before them.

They were silent for a long while, just taking in the scene. When Claire finally tore her gaze away from the lagoon to look at Dex, she was surprised to find that he was already staring at her. She breathed in deeply at the sight of his gorgeous eyes. This only made her irrational and newfound feelings for him intensify, scaring the ever-living shit out of her.

"This is incredible," Dex breathed.

"I've seen this before," she admitted.

"What do you mean?"

"In a vision," she whispered. "I've been seeing this place in my dreams for years. I just can't believe I'm actually here."

"That's your gift?" he asked, true astonishment and wonder in his

35

voice. She couldn't understand why his amazement was for her rather than the beautiful lagoon before them.

She shrugged. "It would seem so."

"That's really cool. I'm glad you could finally make it," he said sincerely, placing his hand on her arm lightly.

"What can you do?" she asked, suddenly curious.

"I have no idea yet. Vincent wasn't very informative when we met on what I could do."

"Oh. He wasn't very informative to me about what this place was, but he was fairly upfront about what I could do."

Dex shrugged. "I don't mind figuring it out on my own."

Every day for the next week they snuck away to the falls. The next time they were on guard duty, they were standing in the river with their pants rolled up to their knees, trying to create water towers. Okay, Claire was trying, Dex was doing.

"You just have to do it like this," he said, creating a perfect column of water in front of him.

Claire's mouth formed a tight line and tried her best to copy him, but ended up splashing herself with water.

A laugh erupted from Dex—he didn't even try to hide it, the bastard. Claire was about to tell him what she thought of that when the duo heard a sudden crack from the woods surrounding them. She snapped her head around, and a circle of pointed rocks instantly surrounded her fist. Dex followed suit, his instincts taking over. They stood in formation, back to back, and started to walk in a circle to evaluate their surroundings.

Claire noticed the wolf before Dex. He was enormous, towering over them. He had marbled grey fur with copper undertones. The wolf snarled at the two of them, and Claire tapped Dex with her free hand.

"Dex, giant wolf," she breathed.

He turned to face the same direction as her. The wolf started to approach slowly, snarling with all of his teeth exposed.

"What do we do? It doesn't seem right to just kill it," Dex said.

Claire didn't think so either. If you could look past the very large and very pointy teeth, he was beautiful. Too beautiful to kill. Despite Claire's desire not to kill the massive wolf, he kept advancing.

Claire's rock spikes sped up in rotating around her fist when Dex yelled, "Stop!"

Claire thought Dex was talking to her, but the wolf suddenly stood down. It knelt in front of Dex, looking up at him obediently.

The rocks around her fist fell away. "What's going on?" Claire muttered.

Dex wasn't listening to her anymore. He stepped towards the wolf, as if he were trying to bargain with him. Slowly, he approached, kneeling in front of the wolf until finally touching the top of his head. Suddenly, it appeared that Dex was in a sort of trance. When he finally looked back at Claire, a giant smile was plastered onto his face.

"His name is Fen," Dex said.

Claire's mouth fell open. "Excuse me?" she sputtered.

"His name is Fen," Dex repeated.

She lifted an eyebrow. "If you name him, you have to keep him," she said dryly, resting a hand on her hip.

Dex gave her a blithe look. "I didn't name him, he already has a name."

"And he told you?" she asked, incredulous.

"Yes," he said, scratching the wolf behind his ears. The wolf's—Fen's—tongue lulled out as he relaxed into Dex's touch.

Finally Dex dropped his hand and Fen started towards Claire. Sure, Fen was playing nice, but he was still a wolf who was taller than her. She wasn't about to go in for a hug. So, she just stood there, her violet eyes wide. Fen's golden eyes bored into hers as he approached. Once he was just in front of her, he leaned in and licked her face.

Claire turned away so fast that she fell flat on her rump, causing Dex to lose himself in his laughter. She scowled at him and waiting for him to get a hold of himself.

"He likes you," he said, wiping away tears.

After Dex calmed down and Claire got back to her feet she looked the pair over. "What do we do with him?" She asked. She suddenly remembered a comment that Vincent made while they were on the monorail to Redwater. "Oh my gods, Dex. You're the beast master!"

Dex—and the wolf—gave her a puzzled look. Wasn't that weird? "Beast master?"

Claire's grin widened. "Vincent told me he had a beast master at the coven. That has to be you."

Fen suddenly looked a little sullen, and Dex started crooning to his wolf. "She doesn't mean you're a beast," he said soothingly.

Claire didn't know if she wanted to laugh or groan.

"Wait," Dex said suddenly. "This means we get to keep him."

"Yeah, I guess," Claire said, scratching her head.

Unbelievably, Fen's tail started wagging. He's a wolf, not a dog, Claire thought. Why is his tail wagging?

Once guard duty was over, Dex excitedly escorted Claire and their new companion to the coven. When they got there, Vincent was already waiting. He already knew what had happened, Claire realized.

"I see you've found your familiar," Vincent said, a prideful gleam in his eye.

Fen's hackles rose when Dex's spine stiffened. Man, those two were really in sync. Once Dex relaxed, his wolf did as well.

"We'll have to find a place for him to sleep," Claire said.

"He can sleep in the cabin," Dex said defensively, and Fen gave Claire an irritated chuff.

She couldn't help but smile at the two of them. They really were cute. "It's not that your furry companion isn't adorable, but I don't think he'll fit through the door."

"He is still a wolf, Dex," Vincent said. There was a light chide to his tone, but he still sounded amused.

Dex eyed Fen for a moment, as if listening to something he was saying, then sighed. "Okay," he relented.

Claire didn't know how her life had changed so drastically in such a short period of time, but she was glad it had.

FOUR

SEVEN YEARS LATER

KATE STOOD IN THE KITCHEN of her modest Lakeshore home. She was chopping up vegetables and adding them to the skillet above the fire to give her mutton just a little more flavor. She smiled as her stomach started to growl. The food smelled amazing, if she did say so herself. While she waited for it to cook, Kate peered out her window. She and her daughter didn't have the largest home in Lakeshore by any means, but she'd bet they had the best view. As the name might suggest, Lakeshore was a city defined by its many lakes, and Kate's house was situated right by one of them. The water always reflected the setting suns, creating the most breathtaking shades of orange and pink.

Kate was also in love with the architecture of Lakeshore. It was why she'd always wanted to move there, especially once she'd met her husband. Lakeshore was on the northwestern tip of Easthaven. Though it was far from Everton, it did share some of Everton's wealth. The homes and buildings had solid metal frames, often on stilts to account for flooding and to accommodate those perfect views. The buildings had a mixture of the industrial styles from Everton, and the more charming feel from the Western cities. The result was a town filled with buildings that all had unique shapes, each with different segments that were rounded or had tall spires. Not to mention the multiple balconies on each floor, as the homes tended to be narrow but tall, and the various sections that jutted out to create cozy sitting areas.

Kate pulled herself from her musings to flip over the two pieces of mutton. It wouldn't be much longer now until the meal was ready. She just hoped that her daughter would get home soon. She was out at the market searching for some new clothes. They'd just had a nice pay day, so Kate could afford to treat her daughter this week. She was just plating the two pieces of meat when the front door slid open.

"Right on time," she called over her shoulder.

Kate expected to hear a happy reply about how great the food smelled or about the nice outfits her daughter had purchased, but instead she heard nothing but the door sliding closed.

Kate walked over to the steps to peer down them, trying to see if Naomi was okay. "Sweetheart?" she called. Still, there was no answer.

Oddly, a light started to wash over the landing. Kate stumbled back a step, trying to shield her eyes.

"Naomi?" she croaked, panic evident in her tone.

The being that turned the corner and started up the steps was not her daughter, that much was clear. That didn't mean that Kate had any idea what it was. The woman, at least she thought it was by the body shape, was absolutely enormous. She was twice as tall as most humans, and she was covered from head to foot in an imposing glow. But that was nothing compared to the eyes. The eyes were a pure bright white, and Kate couldn't bring herself to look at them.

She stumbled backwards, trying to get away from the thing, but it just kept coming. In her desperation, she grabbed a knife and held it in front of her, still unable to look directly at the creature.

"Don't come any closer," she said. She desperately wished that her voice had been strong, but it wasn't. It shook with pure terror.

Kate backed up into the countertop, burning her hand on the fire that was still lit. The knife clattered to the floor as she snatched her hand away and clutched it close to her chest. That moment of distraction was all this being needed. Between one breath and the next it was right in front of her. Kate got out one final gasp of terror before the massive person in front of her plunged a hand into her chest.

Kate wanted to scream as a white hot pain radiated from her chest outwards. It felt like she was burning from the inside out. She couldn't move, couldn't make a noise, could do nothing to get away. She simply stood there, rigid and helpless, as her skin grayed and shriveled. When it was over, Kate was almost unrecognizable. Her skin was thin and dried out, with veins clearly visible on every open surface. Most of her auburn hair had fallen out and her brilliant blue eyes were still and unblinking. Finally, the creature released her, and her body dropped to the floor.

NAOMI HUMMED TO HERSELF as she skipped down the boardwalk towards home. The summer air was damp and cool, smelling like the fresh rainfall. She couldn't wait to show her mother the jewelry she'd bought for her or the new shoes Naomi had purchased for herself. Most of all, she couldn't wait to eat. She hadn't eaten since breakfast, and she was simply ravenous. Not only that, but nothing beat her mother's cooking. She could smell food the moment she neared her house. After she tossed her bag over her shoulder and secured it, Naomi started up the ladder to get inside.

"I'm home!" she called up the stairs. "You'll absolutely love what I got you." Naomi expected a reply, but was met with none. She furrowed her brow and ascended the stairs two at a time, eager to find out what was wrong. When she got to the kitchen, her bag of newly purchased goods dropped to the floor as Naomi rushed to her mother's side.

"Mom?" she screamed as she knelt beside her. This couldn't be her mother. There was no way that this was her mom. Naomi felt her heart shatter into a million pieces as she pulled her mother's decaying head into her lap. Gods, what had happened? Her skin... it was just horrific and hair just kept falling out as Naomi stroked her mother's head and tears dripped down her face. She had to call someone she had to get help maybe someone could fix this someone had to fix it they just had to.

Naomi knew she needed to call for help, but she couldn't bring herself to leave her mother's side. How could she leave her like this? She didn't know how long she sat there for, touching her mother's body and praying to the gods that this was a dream, but finally her eyes started to dry, and her sobs became hoarse.

Suddenly, she got to her feet. She didn't want to get up, but something was pulling at her. It was pulling her out of her house and away from her mother. I can't go, she thought frantically, but that magnetic pull didn't stop. It only got stronger as she stumbled into the night.

FIVE

CLAIRE LET OUT A HEARTY LAUGH. She and Dex were relaxing by the lagoon, basking in the warm suns.

"You cannot be serious," she said.

Dex shrugged. "I'm only telling you what I observe!"

Claire let out a very un-ladylike snort. "She is so not into him."

"I'm telling you she is!"

A sly smile crossed Claire's lips. "Kind of how Blayne is into you?" It was a low blow, Claire knew it was. The frown that crossed Dex's lips caused Dru, the alpha female of Fen's pack, to cast an amused look Claire's way. Her crystal white fur was wet and glistening in the suns. A lot had changed over the past few years. With the addition of Dru, pups had been added to the pack. Dex now had an entire pack of six familiars. In addition, the coven was now at full capacity. Several new interesting members had joined their ranks—including Dex's brothers. That made Claire wonder if magic was genetic. Then there was the arrival of Vlad. Tall with sandy brown hair, deep violet eyes, and a strong affinity for fire. Claire was quite taken with him.

Dex slowly looked away, seeming to drop the subject, but Claire's spine stiffened. She knew very well that he wasn't about to let anything drop. In the next instant, Claire was drenched head to foot in a massive wave of water. Dru jumped up and made a disgruntled noise, and Claire scrambled to her feet. Upon attempting that, however, she slipped and tumbled into the lagoon. If she wasn't already soaked, she would have been mad. Thankfully, it was well into summer so the water was rather warm. Her head broke the surface to see Dex looming over her, laughter in his ocean blue eyes. He held a cordial hand out to Claire and she took it. If she caused a pillar of rocks to rise under his feet and knock him into the water, well, there wasn't much she could do about that.

Finally, they both got out of the water and started to dry off. Without warning, Claire's eyes went pure black, causing Dex to jump up and grab her shoulders.

"Claire?" he yelled, but she didn't respond. She just sat rigid in his bruising grip.

The vision came in flashes. She saw a pair of ice blue eyes and heard laughter. Half of that laughter was hers, but half of it wasn't. A feeling of pure warmth washed over her, and she felt truly happy. Claire wanted to stay here, but her vision had other ideas. It dragged her away from the laughter and warmth until she was in the center of the coven. She couldn't see it very clearly, but she knew where she was nonetheless. The table just had an energy that nothing else did. She saw a tall, masculine form atop it. That was Vincent. No mistaking him. His height gave him away. Next to him was a woman. She was tall, but so was every other woman in the coven.

Claire's heart sped up as a deep feeling of dread fell over her. The woman got down on her knees and rested her head on some kind of block. She really wanted to see who it was, but everything was still so blurry. Vincent changed his position until he was facing her. He pulled something out of his belt, and it elongated as it flashed in the light. That couldn't be what she thought it was. There was no way. And there was no way he was about to—

Vincent lifted the sword and swung it downwards in a graceful arc. Claire couldn't help but watch in abject horror as the sword cut cleanly through the woman's neck and her head fell from her body. There was blood everywhere. Claire started forwards, trying to see who that was; but she was sucked backwards into the present.

44

She couldn't stabilize her breathing for the life of her. It felt like she was having a panic attack, her heart was racing and she was hyperventilating. Her eyes rolled back in her head, as she fainted in Dex's arms.

NAOMI RAN THROUGH THE WOODS, scraping her arms on the trees surrounding her. She couldn't feel the pain, though. Her body was on autopilot. She couldn't feel or hear anything except for the faint calling of her voice to somewhere—she didn't even know where. Not that she cared; she was too devastated to care about anything. She didn't want to wake up from whatever trance she was in.

She only wanted to not be alone.

DEX LIFTED CLAIRE IN HIS ARMS and manipulated the air around them to lift him to the top of the cliff. He was extremely thankful that he spent these years honing his abilities for all elements, not just earth. He started to sprint back to camp while still keeping Claire as still as he could.

He was terrified that he was too late as he finally entered the courtyard. People immediately took notice as he came in and set her down on the table.

"Farrah! I need you. Someone get Vincent!" He yelled, his heart pounding. She still wasn't moving. He'd seen her have visions before, but they'd never done this to her.

Farrah ran to them immediately, placing her hand on Claire's forehead. She closed her eyes and focused her energy.

Dex stiffened when he saw the figure approaching them. Vlad was the same height as Dex, but he wasn't as broad or well built. He had sandy brown hair that was always messy in a purposeful way, and he had bright violet eyes that were only a shade darker than Claire's. Dex knew that was what Vlad and Claire had bonded over when

45

they first met a few years ago, and it only snowballed from there. He felt a sort of...jealousy towards him, but that was hardly relevant right now.

"What happened?" Vlad asked urgently.

"She passed out. I think she had a vision."

Farrah nodded. "Whatever this is, it isn't medical. I can't help her."

Dex's eyes went wild with panic at Farrah's words as Vincent approached.

"What's going on?" he asked.

"We were out, and her eyes went black. Once they went back to normal, she wasn't breathing right and passed out," Dex explained.

"I've seen this before. She'll wake up when her body's recovered. The vision must have been substantial." Vincent sighed and thought for a moment. "Dex, take her to her room and come to me immediately when she wakes up."

Dex nodded as he picked Claire up and took her to her cabin.

Blayne was sitting on the couch as he walked in, immediately perking up. Once she realized what was happening, her face was coated with worry. "What happened?" she asked.

"She passed out from a vision. I'm to stay with her until she wakes up." He walked straight to her door and magically opened it. He slowly laid her down on her bed.

"Well, we can wait out in the living room until she wakes up...if you want," Blayne said with a sad smile.

"I can't," he said, his voice as sincere as he could muster.

She pinched her face together. "Of course. I'll be out here if you need anything." She retreated back into the living room.

Dex looked at the sleeping Claire and felt his heart drop. Her breathing was shallow and she didn't stir as he brushed the hair out of her face. He knew this was normal, but he couldn't help but be terribly worried.

After what felt like forever, her eyes opened.

"Hey," Dex said softly.

"Hey," Claire said, voice straining. "What happened?"

"That's the million dollar question. Your eyes went black, and then you passed out."

Claire thought hard for a moment as the vision rushed back to her. She wasn't sure if she should tell anyone what she saw. Vincent was executing someone with some sort of...sword. It wasn't made of metal, but it was unmistakable. That wasn't a normal sword. She couldn't focus too much on the sword, though, because Vincent was going to kill someone.

Granted, Claire knew that whenever a new coven member came in, one had to die. She didn't recognize the flashing face from her vision, so she assumed a new member was coming. If only she could see the face of the one who'd die in her place... It obviously wasn't Claire, since she was observing the scene, so that gave her some relief. Claire found herself wondering who the weakest link in the coven was, but then decided she didn't even want to think about the scene she'd witnessed in her vision. How soon would this happen, though?

Claire shook her head, mostly at herself.

"Are you okay?" He asked.

Claire looked at him and sighed. "I think so. I was just overwhelmed."

"What happened?"

"I—I should talk to Vincent."

"You're right. He told me to get him once you woke up, so I'll get him. If you need me, I'll be right outside your cabin," he said, his tone unusually serious.

"Dex, I'm fine. I promise. If I need you, I'll find you."

He nodded and gave Claire a heartfelt look before standing and leaving her room. Only a few moments later, Vincent walked in.

"How are you?" He asked, sitting down next to her on the bed.

"I'm okay now. It was my first major vision while being awake, so I guess my body didn't know how to handle it."

He nodded. "What happened in it?"

Claire took a deep breath. "I saw a new member come in, then a very graphic scene of you... taking care of the member she replaces."

Vincent nodded, not seeming at all surprised. "So, a new member is coming soon then. Did anything else happen to give you a clue as to who's coming or going?"

Claire shook her head. "I saw flashes of the girl's face who's coming in, but I can't remember it clearly enough to tell you anything about her other than her sex. You had a weird... sword?"

Vincent nodded. "My affinity is for air. When executions happen, I use a sword made of air. All coven leaders do it that way."

Claire imagined fire, water, and earth swords in her mind. They all sounded cool in theory, but to know they're used for executing coven members… "Well that makes some things clearer," she whispered.

Vincent sighed. "I'm glad it was nothing worse than that. With the stress it put on your body, I was worried."

Had she been younger, Claire might have been more shocked. Nevertheless, she wasn't. Though the images had been graphic, they'd all known what being in a coven meant. She shook her head. "Nothing more than routine, I guess."

"It's a big deal," he said, "since this is the first new member we'll have since reaching capacity." He stood up slowly.

Claire nodded. "Is there anything else you need?"

Vincent shook his head. "Thank you, and keep resting up for a little bit."

Claire nodded again, willing him to leave. She felt deadly exhausted, but a wave of relief went over her as she saw the next person entering her room.

"You scared us quite a bit, Claire," Vlad said softly. He came and sat next to her on the bed, grabbing her hand. When Vlad came to the coven, they'd immediately become friends. Over the past few years, that friendship evolved into something more. Claire wasn't quite sure what was happening between the two of them, but that was okay. She had a thousand years to decide what she wanted, and she was in no rush.

"Sorry, I thought things were just too comfortable here. We needed a good scare," Claire joked.

"Ha. Ha. Ha. Not funny. When Farrah said it wasn't medical, my heart dropped. I thought we were gonna have to slap you awake or something. Or drop you from the top of a tree to wake your ass up."

Claire laughed. "You're ridiculous. You'd get murdered if you tried to drop me from a tree." She imagined the scene, Vlad having her in his arms at the top of the tallest tree in the forest. She imagined Dex at the bottom, just screaming at Vlad to get her down safely, surrounded by his wolves. They'd all be snarling at Vlad, probably trying to rip him to shreds by the time they reached the bottom.

"You're probably right," Vlad laughed. "What happened?" His voice got sincere with the question.

Claire gulped. She didn't want to recount the information again. She squeezed his hand and said, "Someone new is coming. I saw someone get...executed? Gods, that sounds so morbid."

"Wow, that's heavy. No wonder you passed out. I'm so sorry you had to see that," he whispered.

"It's okay. There's obviously a reason I had to see it. It is our first new member, so that's kind of a huge deal. I just wonder who the new girl is."

Vlad let out an exaggerated sigh of relief. "Well, it's good to know I won't be murdered."

Claire laughed. He always had a way of making her laugh in the most horrible situations. "And I won't, since I was the one observing it. I just hope it's not Farrah. Is that bad to say? That that's the first person I'd want to save?"

Vlad let out a hearty laugh. "Honestly, no. Farrah is the best member we have. After the two of us, of course."

"Oh, you're so right. The coven would fall apart completely without her."

They laughed again, then Claire's head had a shooting pain through it. She grabbed her forehead and sighed, trying to laugh it off.

"You need some rest," Vlad said, "as much as I love joking about one of our coven members dying."

Claire gave him a small smile. "You're right. Thanks for coming to see me."

He squeezed her hand again before releasing it. "Of course. I'll see you tomorrow. Rest up, and please, never scare me like that again."

Claire nodded. After he left, she fell asleep almost immediately.

NAOMI WAS STILL RUNNING THROUGH THE WOODS. How long had she been running? How far? Where was she going? She was slowly starting to come to, wondering what the hell was going on. Where the hell was she?

It was night time, she finally realized. She could see almost as well as in the day time. That was new. What was happening to her? Her mother died, then suddenly she was out the door. It was like an internal switch flipped, and suddenly she wasn't herself anymore. She was a pawn being called somewhere that wasn't home.

She was terrified.

She wanted to stop.

She wanted to go home.

CLAIRE WAS ASLEEP WHEN THE SCREAMING STARTED. She shot up in bed and glanced around her room, wondering what was going on. She went into the living room where Blayne was tying her boot laces.

"What's happening?" Claire asked, rubbing her eyes.

"Intruder, apparently. I don't see why anyone would want to intrude here," she said far too casually for the situation.

Claire's heart started to pound. 'Intruders' weren't really possible. Humans walked right through this place and only a potential coven member could enter. Surely Blayne knew that. That said, the revelations from her vision hadn't been made public, that much was obvious, so Claire played it cool. There had to be some reason why Vincent was withholding information.

"That's weird. Hang on, let me just grab some shoes and a jacket." Claire went back into her room to get fully ready, then came back into the living room.

"You ready?" Blayne asked.

"Let's go."

Protocol for an intruder was simple. Once the intruder was spotted by someone on guard duty, they were to return to the heart of the coven immediately to alert Vincent. Vincent would then assemble all twenty-eight members to stand behind their respective cabins, wielding their elements. Who ever saw the intruder first would alert the rest of coven—mostly Vincent—and identify if the intruder was a threat. If so, necessary action would be taken under Vincent's orders.

Claire and Blayne took their spots behind their cabin. Claire made rock arrows that hovered around both of her fists, while Blayne created a circle of flames that encircled hers. They stood there for a while in silence until Blayne spoke.

"Gods, if this is a false alarm I'm going to fight Vincent personally," she said bitterly.

"I don't know, he doesn't seem like the type for false alarms," Claire whispered, jaw tight.

"Maybe not, but nothing's happening. I doubt there's even a real intruder. It's probably just one of Dex's wolves running around, and one of the newbies doesn't recognize them from first glance. So he got scared and came crying to Vincent, and here I am, not getting my well-deserved sleep."

"Blayne, be a little more serious about this."

"Just watch, hon, I'm right. It's nothing huge," she whispered.

A scream erupted on the other side of the camp. Claire and Blayne shot their heads around, both of their elements growing stronger. They ran to the source of the scream, making it before Vincent arrived.

A girl was standing there, her face covered in worry and pure terror. She had a sweet, heart-shaped face with icy blue eyes that were glowing intensely. Her eyes were hooded and fairly thin, but with their color, they stood out. Her hair was a deep auburn, and she had a long but small, button nose with a full mouth that was agape. Claire thought that she was only a year or so younger than her, but something about this newcomer seemed familiar. There was something else, too.

This girl seemed... powerful and like she knew more than she should. She was short—and she would have been short in the outside world—but her eyes were unmistakable in their glow. It looked like she was out of breath. Claire found herself feeling unnecessarily antsy and scared, as if she was feeling the same things she was. The girl suddenly locked eyes with Claire and something passed between them. A mutual understanding of sorts.

The entire coven stood at attention, ready to fire against this poor girl. Claire didn't want to, though. She looked innocent and scared, not like she was here to ruin the safety of the coven.

Claire suddenly realized. The girl's eyes.

She knew those eyes.

Vincent arrived, finally, and yelled, *"STOP!"*

SIX

VINCENT RAN UP TO THE GIRL standing in front of all of the coven members and stopped a few feet in front of her. All of the worry immediately drained from her face and was quickly replaced with a deep sadness along with a bittersweet smile.

"Dad?" The girl said, just loud enough for Claire to hear.

Dad? Vincent had a daughter? Why was she here? Why did he leave her? A million questions ran through Claire's mind, as a wave of bittersweet joy hit her. Why was she having these weird feelings? It wasn't like she knew this woman.

"Naomi, gods, what are you doing here?" He immediately took her into his arms and gave her a strong hug. A wave of pure happiness radiated from the scene. Claire glanced at Blayne to see if she had the same confused look on her face.

"Do you feel that?" Claire asked.

"Yeah, it's like emotional control or something. Must be her," Blayne whispered.

"Naomi, you've got to control your power," Vincent said, loud enough for the whole coven to hear. Claire figured that was his way of explaining why the coven was feeling these odd emotional changes.

She was more interested in knowing finding out more about the girl from her vision, beyond the fact that she was Vincent's daughter.

Naomi was still breathing heavily when Vincent pulled away. "Did you run all the way from Lakeshore?" he asked, keeping his voice low.

Naomi stared up at him, her hands shaking. "I—I guess. I don't remember a lot. I just—oh, Dad, something horrible happened."

Vincent turned around to the rest of the coven before looking back to Naomi. He nodded and whispered, "Let me handle them, then we can talk downstairs."

"Downstairs?" she asked.

Vincent nodded before turning to the rest of the coven. When he spoke, his voice was amplified. "Everyone, this is Naomi. She is no intruder, she is a new member seeking refuge. You know what happens when new members come in, and we will deal with this in a timely manner. As for tonight, everyone report back to bed or back to guard duty. I will see all of you at breakfast."

He gave a stern nod to the coven members, and they started to disperse. Claire lingered for a moment, staring at the girl from her vision—at Naomi. Her eyes were ethereal in how much they glowed. From the glow of her eyes, Claire figured she had a stronger connection with the coven or power in general. She figured the latter, considering she could easily manipulate the emotions of the entire coven without even trying.

Claire finally turned on the ball of her foot and followed Blayne back to their cabin.

"Now what?" Blayne hissed, sounding nervous.

Claire swallowed hard and shrugged as she waved open the door to their cabin. "I don't know… I mean I do—"

"Well, yeah," Blayne agreed. "We all do."

"But not really," Claire added as the door slid closed behind them.

Vincent and Naomi stood there until everyone had left. "Follow me," he said. He led her to the table and stood next to it, closing his eyes and spreading it in half with just a gesture. A spiral staircase appeared under the table, and Vincent led Naomi to his chambers.

His chambers were simple. There was a comfortable seating area combined with a kitchen and what looked to be the door to a washroom. On the right, there was a guest bedroom of sorts. That was for new coven members. They stayed there until the trial and execution. After that, they moved into their cabin. Directly across from the entrance there was another door that led to Vincent's room.

Naomi nervously glanced around, trying to get her bearings. The room felt too dark and cramped, and her deep sorrow was overwhelming.

"What happened, sweetheart?" Vincent asked softly, drawing Naomi's attention.

Naomi paused for a moment, in total awe at the situation. She stared at her father. He looked the same. He shouldn't. He should have deeper laugh lines and crow's feet. His hair should be thinner and have more touches of gray. His gate should be less confident and his musculature should be starting to decay. Yet, it wasn't. He looked frozen in time. It was jarring. She shook her head quickly, "Sorry, I just can't believe I ran to your coven."

Vincent's face fell. "I'm sorry."

She turned away, unable to watch her father. She thought she might have been able to handle this—seeing Vincent again—under normal circumstances. But with her mother dead…

"We understood. This is what you had to do, and we knew it'd happen eventually," she said, trying to keep her voice steady. Vincent had always felt the draw of a coven. Her mother hadn't believed it at first, but she'd come to understand. Naomi had grown up with the knowledge that one day her father would be drawn away by some invisible force.

"I missed you so much, Naomi." He gave her another strong hug, squeezing her towards the end of it.

"I missed you too, Dad."

"How's Mom?" He asked, eyes full of hope.

Naomi wanted nothing more than to lie to him. She wanted to tell him that Kate was safe at home, missing them dearly but still alive. Her heart ached at the words she was about to say.

"That's why I'm here, I think. She—something—I don't know, Dad." Naomi broke out into a sob.

Vincent held her closer as she cried, already knowing what she was going to say. "How did it happen?" he asked softy. He was doing

55

everything he could not to break. He hadn't seen his wife in seven years, but he loved her more with every day he couldn't see her. He had this plan that he was going to bring her in once the coven was established—once it was safe for her. He was the leader, he could do whatever he wanted, even if it was unconventional.

He would go back to Lakeshore, walk into their home, and open his arms. She was going to run into them. Then he was going to take her home.

Kate... his heart shattered into a million pieces.

"I have no idea. I went out shopping, then when I came back she was on the floor. It looked like the life had been sucked out of her. She was grey—her hair—she—Dad, I can't, I'm sorry," she sobbed.

He shook his head, holding back tears. "You're fine, honey. You're safe. You don't have to talk anymore. I'm here. We're okay. We're..." he drifted off.

He knew what killed her, but he wouldn't say a word more about it.

"What could have done this to her?" Naomi sobbed.

Vincent let out a shaky breath. "Let's get you to bed, sweetheart. You must be exhausted. Come, I have a room over here where new members can sleep." He led her to a room on the right, opening the door with a mere gesture.

Naomi nodded. "I love you, Dad."

"I love you, too. Try to get some sleep. I'll wake you up for breakfast in the morning."

CLAIRE BARELY SLEPT THROUGH THE NIGHT. She was reeling from what happened, millions of questions were scattering through her mind. When it was time for breakfast, she got dressed and went outside to see almost everyone gathered already. Vincent and Naomi were standing off to the side together. She looked tired and terrified. Claire was sure there was a reason, other than the fact that she ran here all the way from Lakeshore. That was no small distance. But, she was also sure that this place wasn't a huge shock if her father was running it. She looked away from the duo with a small jump.

Vlad placed a light hand on Claire's back. "Is that?"

Claire looked at him, a surprised look on her face. "Yeah, that's her."

Vlad paled. He knew what it meant. Someone was about to die. Maybe not today, but soon.

DEX WAS ACROSS FROM CLAIRE, flanked by Fen and Dru when she finally met his eyes. He strode over to her, and Claire didn't miss the fact that Fen stepped between her and Vlad while Dru nuzzled her face. She smiled weakly as she ran a hand through her fur. The wolves loved Claire, but they were never really friendly with anyone other than she and Dex.

"What did you see yesterday?" Dex whispered under the cover of his familiars.

Claire looked around, most of the coven wasn't focused on her, but she didn't want to change that.

"Let's go inside," she said.

Blayne gave them an inquisitive look as Claire led Dex to their cabin. Dex gave a stern nod to his familiars, and they scattered into the woods. Once inside, she rested her hip against the grand piano. "The vision. It was of that new girl."

He ran a hand over his face. "Vincent's daughter?"

She nodded. "That's not all..." she trailed off, swallowing hard. "I saw someone being beheaded. I couldn't tell who it was; I just know that it wasn't me."

The color drained from Dex's face, but he looked relieved at the same time. They'd all known that this would happen in the coven one day. Every coven went through this. They went through it for a thousand years before everything was settled. That didn't mean that the first time would be easy.

"That's..." Dex trailed off, unsure of what to say.

"Yeah. I just didn't think she'd arrive so soon. I thought we'd have time to prepare."

"Well, it looks like Vincent was certainly surprised. Did you not tell him about your vision?"

"I did," Claire said incredulously, "I guess he just wasn't expecting his own daughter to show up."

"None of us did. Did you even know that he had a child? Or really a life outside of here?"

Claire shrugged. "I never thought about it, really. I guess I kind of assumed his life started here. I just can't imagine him leaving his family."

"I feel bad for his wife. Her husband and child both left for coven life."

"It wasn't voluntary," she said, giving him a meaningful look. Dex knew that. Greg and Jorgen had been drawn towards the coven before Vincent had even found them. "He didn't tell me how he got here, but I can't imagine anyone leaving their family willingly."

"I can't either. I know when Vincent came for me, it felt like I had no choice." Dex sighed. Claire knew that leaving his brothers behind was hard. Luckily for him, both Greg and Jorgen had joined three years ago as the two final members of the coven. "We should get back out there. Vincent's going to have to make an announcement, I'm sure."

Almost like clockwork, Vincent's voice started booming out as they exited the cabin.

"We have a new member coming into our coven. Her name is Naomi, and, yes, she is my daughter. This does not mean I will treat her differently when it comes to coven proceedings. She will be treated like the rest of you. With the arrival of a new coven member, there comes a trial. Males, you are obviously exempt from this trial. You will still be present, but not directly involved.

"Women, you will be called up to the table for the trial. I will be evaluating each of you by use of magic, including Naomi. The weakest will be executed, even if the weakest turns out to be the newcomer. The execution will be done by a sword.

"I apologize for being blunt, but this is the reality of our society. In order for us to survive and make it to a thousand years, we need the strongest members. It is also a way of evaluating the progress of our coven, for everyone should be stronger before the next new member comes in. If anyone has any questions, I will be willing to answer them, but a lot of it comes from the experience itself. The trial will come five days from now." Vincent stepped down from the table, Naomi following suit.

Naomi's heart was pounding. She didn't want all of this attention, especially with her swollen eyes, red nose, and cheeks. Her chest ached, especially knowing someone would now have to die for her to be at home here. She'd had enough death for the past few days, and she wasn't going to be ready for any more for another lifetime.

She started to look around at the coven members. Many of them were in little groups. There were two people, a man and a woman, standing and smiling with each other. He had darker hair and skin, while she had pale skin with red hair. They seemed very in sync with each other, like they spent a lot of time together. She also noticed a young pair of twins sitting in the dirt looking uneasy.

She was starting to feel how short she was when looking around as well. She'd always been used to her father being a foot and a half taller than her, but even here, everyone had at least six inches on her. Her eyes landed on two huge wolves, even taller than her father. There were three people standing around the wolves, with a fourth approaching slowly.

The girl approaching set her arm on a man's bicep. As his head turned, the wolves' heads turned as well to look at the girl. He looked annoyed by her touch, immediately looking at the other girl across from him. She also had a man standing next to her. They were close together, and with a movement of his hand towards her, the smaller of the two wolves moved against the girl, catching her attention.

Naomi laughed to herself at the scene. She stared at the four of them, feeling a pang of loss. They looked so content with their lives here, not a shred of sadness between them. She envied that, especially right now. Her father had told her stories of covens as she was growing up, and she always knew he was going to one day leave to establish one. She only went to bed every night praying she could go with him, but she didn't want to be with him like this. Not with her mother shriveled on the floor of their old home.

She found herself wondering what would happen to her body. It appeared as if she was going to turn to dust after a short while. Or what if someone found her? What would they do? What would they think? Naomi knew she was safe here, no one could find her even if they thought she was capable of doing that to her mother. She didn't want to think about it anymore. She looked back up to the group of four.

Suddenly, a hand was placed on her elbow, causing her to jump. "Hello, darling, how are you doing?" a woman with a very sweet face asked. She radiated healing energy and a kind heart, something that Naomi truly needed during this time.

"H-hi," she stammered. "I'm well," she said softly.

The woman gave her an apologetic smile. "I'm Farrah. Your father's told me all about you."

Naomi couldn't help but give her a soft smile. "It's nice to meet you, Farrah. I'm Naomi."

"It's a pleasure to finally meet you. Would you like me to introduce you to some people?"

Naomi nodded. "That would be nice." Farrah must've seen the lost look in her eyes and felt bad for her. Naomi didn't mind. She loved the company.

"This is May and Sam," she said as they approached the duo she was looking at earlier.

"Hey," they said in unison.

"They're on guard duty together, so don't be surprised when they're a little too in sync," Farrah said with a laugh.

They moved on to other members of the coven until landing on the group of four that Naomi was drawn to.

"This is Blayne, Dex, Vlad, and Claire. The wolves are Fen and Dru," Farrah gestured to each of them as she stated their names.

Naomi smiled at each one, her eyes landing finally on Claire. She was a bit taller than her and gave off a hard energy, but the longer Naomi read her the more she saw her caring side. She had vibrant violet eyes with dark brown hair that had a purple undertone. It was wavy and ended at the top of her chest. She had a defined jawline and arched cheekbones, with a poised mouth and long, defined nose. One of her eyebrows seemed to be permanently raised, giving her face a sarcastic feel. Her eyes were narrowed and her pupils dilated, also giving her a scared look. Naomi chuckled to herself, seeing right through that. She could see who a person really was, and Claire's facial expression did not match what Naomi could see. She couldn't quite figure out why she looked scared, though.

Naomi looked through the rest of the group, giving them a small smile. "Hi, everyone," she said softly.

They all gave her polite smiles, including Claire. That scared look didn't leave her eyes through her smile.

"Welcome to the coven," Vlad said, holding his hand out. He radiated a kind energy.

She took it and shook his hand firmly. "Thanks. Whose are these?" she asked, gesturing to the wolves.

Dex, the man with tanned skin and ocean, blue eyes grinned. "They're some of my familiars. They can't stand to be away from me for more than five minutes, while the other four like to adventure. You'll see them around." He had a proud look in his eyes when talking about his familiars. Naomi could read the love in his heart as well as the cold energy he held.

Blayne gave her a sardonic grin. She seemed nice enough, but there was something shy about her.

"It's really nice to meet you all," Naomi said.

Claire's eyes narrowed on her. This was surreal for her. Just yesterday, she was seeing flashes of her face. She remembered the carefree feeling of pure joy associated with her face, but this girl's arrival would also be responsible for the upcoming death of one of the people she considered family.

SEVEN

A COUPLE DAYS LATER, Claire was relaxing in the summer heat when she noticed Naomi sitting by a tree.

Claire still felt odd about seeing her face in real life now, even though she'd seen it for the first time only days ago. She looked lonely, beyond the fact that she was physically alone. Claire sighed and sat up from the bench before sauntering over to Naomi.

"Adjusting okay?" she asked.

Naomi looked up suddenly, and an acute wave of fear washed over Claire. Naomi really needed to calm down with that influencing of hers, then realized that she probably had no clue how. That was nothing to be mad at her for.

"It's okay, the people have been nice so far." Naomi was again startled as one of the large wolves, Dru, appeared from the forest.

Another wave of emotion hit Claire, despite the fact that she trusted Dru with her life.

"Is she yours?" Naomi asked, standing up. Even if Claire hadn't felt her nervousness, she would have known. Naomi looked properly spooked.

Claire shrugged, doing her best to appear casual. She figured that if she were calm, Naomi might calm down, too. "No, she's Dex's. He's a beast master, and she's one of his familiars, but she always follows me around. I don't really know why, but I don't mind."

Dru stood protectively next to Claire. She gave a small laugh to the mountain of a wolf, "She's fine, Dru. She's nice. We like her. Go on, see."

Dru looked between the two of them before stepping towards Naomi, giving her a few small sniffs. She started to circle around her, dragging her tail across her body, and causing Naomi to jump a little. Once Dru made a decision, she put her face close to Naomi and gave her a small kiss.

"Good girl," Claire said, petting Dru once she settled into her spot next to her.

"She's absolutely gorgeous," Naomi said, astonished. She obviously was terrified of these creatures, because who wouldn't be? They were massive.

"I credit her good behavior all to me. You should see the other wolves that Dex has raised, they are all troublemakers who just run around the woods all day. Other than Fen, though. He doesn't leave Dex's side."

"That's sweet," she paused, "and a really awesome power to have, honestly. I'd love to have a bunch of cats following me around everywhere," she chuckled.

Claire chuckled. "No, no, these dogs reign supreme. If we ever had a real invasion, they'd prove very useful for all of us."

"So would cats! They could distract everyone with their cuteness then strike when the invaders least expect it."

Claire laughed. "Okay, I guess you've got me there. Do you want me to show you around a little bit?"

Naomi looked around. "I've seen everything outside, but I have no idea what the inside of one of these cabins looks like."

Claire was puzzled for a moment, then remembered that new members stayed with Vincent until a room in a cabin was open to them. Claire nodded. "Okay, follow me. I'll show you where I live." She led her to the other side of the coven and stopped in front of her door.

"Dru, girl, you know you can't follow me in here. These doors aren't big enough for you," she said.

A whimper came from Dru, then she simply laid down next to Claire's front door.

"You're ridiculous, cutie," Claire said, petting her head. She opened her French doors with a gesture, leading Naomi inside.

"Welcome to my humble abode," she said with a smile.

Naomi glanced around, her eyes finally settling on the grand piano in the front of the room. For the first time since she'd arrived, true excitement washed over her—and Claire—causing one of Claire's eyebrows to rise.

"Oh, that's so cool, do you play?" Naomi asked, dragging her hand across the smooth, white surface.

Claire gave a small chuckle. "No, it was there before I even got here."

Naomi gave her an odd look. "Why? Does your roommate play?"

Claire shook her head. "If I could tell you, I would. She said it was here when she arrived as well."

Naomi laughed, a twinkle in her bright, blue eyes. "Well, at least someone in this coven now knows how to play." Naomi sat down at the bench in front of the piano and started to play a gorgeous song. She looked at home while playing, and the feeling of nostalgia came over Claire. A warm smile sat on her face.

Once Naomi was finished, she was smiling radiantly.

"That was amazing," Claire gasped.

"Thank you, it's my mother's favorite," Naomi said, her smile turning sad.

Claire sobered. "I'm sure you miss her. What's she like?"

Naomi gave her another small smile. "She's gorgeous, inside and out. She's an amazing cook, much better than this food they serve here. Not that the food here is bad," she babbled in a panic.

"No offense taken," Claire said gently. "Home cooked meals are always better."

Naomi gave her a grateful look. "Anyway, I wish she could've come. But I guess she never had the 'gene' or whatever causes us to be this way."

Claire nodded, wanting to know more about what life was like when Vincent and Naomi left. Obviously, it was way too soon to ask a perfect stranger that question. "Well, she sounds awesome," Claire said, not really knowing how else to respond.

Naomi nodded, a sadness permeating through the room as her face fell and her eyes landed on the floorboards.

"Why don't we go talk to some people? Or do training?" Claire asked, trying to shake Naomi's melancholy state. She couldn't stand to be around sadness, it made her uncomfortable. Also, this pitiful girl was just ripped from her home and would now be responsible for the first death of their coven. That would be hard on anyone.

"Sure, I'd like to meet some people. I think Dad wants to start training with me so he can feel all... fatherly," Naomi said. She was ecstatic that she was with her father, especially after thinking that she was never going to see him again, but that didn't lessen the pain of her mother's... passing. She didn't think anything was going to, but she welcomed the distraction that Claire wanted to bring her.

Claire led her back outside to the courtyard and walked straight up to the red-headed girl Naomi had seen the morning after she arrived. She was missing her normal companion.

"May, you've met Naomi, right?" Claire asked.

"Only briefly, how do you do?" May said with a bright smile, and her voice was soft and coated in an accent. She was definitely older than Naomi, probably somewhere in her mid-thirties, and her face was coated in freckles. She had a perfectly rounded nose and a small mouth to match, with different colored glowing eyes. One was a bright teal; the other was the same color as tree bark. She was a bit taller than Claire, maybe by a few inches, and was very muscular compared to the rest of the women. Naomi looked down to May's hands to see that one was replaced by a mechanical replica that disappeared into her sleeve. She kept her eyes from widening at the scene. Though Easthaven was a rich and bountiful region, this technology was native to Solaris. Her left hand was adorned by a plain ring on her third finger, another item that was akin with Solaris. Naomi saw a great pain in her heart, overwhelmed by her thriving optimism, a clash of emotions that took Naomi by surprise. She smelled the same as Claire, like the trees that surrounded them.

Naomi did her best to squash her nervousness and plaster on a smile. "Great, yourself?"

May shrugged. "I can't complain, things are pretty good around here."

"So, you're from Solaris, yes?" Naomi asked suddenly.

May gave her a knowing smile. "Yes, you obviously know your regions well."

"My father was always well-travelled, telling me stories of all of the major countries when I was growing up. I know Solaris is known for their meat exports and medical feats, and the ring you're wearing a staple for wedding accessories there."

May looked impressed by Naomi's wealth of knowledge. "Not many people here know much of Solaris. I didn't even know Vincent had visited there before he found me."

Naomi nodded. "He and my mother travelled a lot before I was born. You should ask him about it at some point, I'm sure he'd love to relay his adventures."

She smiled at Naomi and gave her a nod. "I just might. It was a pleasure talking to you, dear." May walked towards her cabin.

"O-okay," Naomi said, wavering.

Claire laid a gentle hand on Naomi's arm. "Don't mind her. She's really anti-social sometimes, so it's normal for her to just leave in the middle of conversations," Claire whispered. She started to look around for more people to talk to before her eyes settled on a...lovely set of twins.

"Come, I'll introduce you to Dex's brothers. They're only thirteen, so try not to take them too seriously. They're also kind of assholes," she continued.

Naomi let out a laugh, knowing Claire meant what she said, but she meant it in a loving way. "Yeah, yeah, okay. I'll put up a mental shield. Anything else I should know about them?"

"Yeah, Greg's older by seven minutes. Jorgen wants to forget that. Greg won't let him. Let's hope like hell that wears off in a few years. Let's go." Claire led her over to the twins, who were standing by their cabin petting one of Dex's familiars.

"Hey, guys, have you met Naomi?" Claire said with the kindest voice she could muster. Copper noticed her and rubbed his head against her shoulder. She smiled and laid a hand on the side of his neck. Copper was much smaller than Fen or Dru because he was only two years old. His copper colored coat was why Dex had named him that. Usually, the wolves were named by their parents (Fen and Dru), but that time they had let Dex do the naming.

CLAIRE HAD BEEN LYING AGAINST DRU at the tree line when she jumped up, causing Claire's head to collide with the tree behind them. Dru started whimpering and limped towards Dex's cabin.

"Dex! I think Dru's about to give birth!" Claire yelled. During her pregnancy, Dru stuck close to Claire. She was only around Dex when he summoned her.

He ran to his familiar's side and followed her. Dex's cabin doors were replaced with ones that could accommodate his pack after Dru and Fen started to mate. Claire was close behind and shut the doors behind the three of them.

"She probably wants to be alone right now," Claire said. She knew Dex was going to ignore her like he always did when it came to Dru's pups, but she felt like she still needed to try.

Like she expected, he sat down next to Dru as she curled up on the floor.

The labor and litter size for these wolves was different from for wild ones. Dru was always pregnant for the same about of time, but when she retreated to Dex's cabin they knew that the pup would arrive within an hour. They knew that she was only minutes out when Fen slapped his tail against the front door and stood guard there. Unlike normal wolves, she has only given birth to one or two pups per litter.

"You think I'm going to leave her at a time like this? I'm becoming a grandfather. Again," Dex said sternly.

Claire chuckled and started walking towards Dex's room. "I'll get the towels," she said with a shake of her head.

They sat together like this for a while until they heard Fen's tail hit the front door. Dex's face was coated in excitement, a wide smile taking over. New pups were not only incredibly adorable, but it was a time of celebration for the whole coven.

Right as Dru gave birth, Dex wrapped the pup with a towel and took him to Dru's face. She then licked him clean to expose his gorgeous copper fur, complimenting the undertones in Fen's own fur.

Fen then knocked his tail against the door rapidly, and Dex let him in. Claire stepped back as the four of them sat together.

Dex looked up suddenly and said, "They want me to name him. They said that he's the last of the pack, so they're letting me name him this time."

Claire's jaw dropped. They had three other pups by this time, and the naming of them was almost like a ritual for Fen and Dru. "That's incredible," she breathed.

"How about Rover?" Dex asked excitedly.

Claire gave him a pointed look. "You're kidding, right?" Dru was also giving him a glare.

"Are you serious? That's an adorable name!" He exclaimed.

"This is why they don't let you name their children," Claire said, rolling her eyes.

"Fine, fine, okay. Howly?" he asked with a large, toothy smile.

Dru laid her head down against her paws, and even Fen turned away from Dex. Claire laughed, "I don't think they like that one either. What about something for his fur? It's incredibly unique compared to his brothers'."

Dex snapped his fingers. "You're right! How about Bronze?" After the wolves gave no reaction to that name, Dex tried again by timidly saying, "Copper?"

Fen and Dru turned their heads back to Dex in unison before they both started to groom their newest son.

Claire gave him a warm smile as she walked to over to the family and started to slowly present her hand towards the newborn.

"May I?" she asked Fen.

He stepped backwards, signaling that she could touch the new pup.

Dex's smile hadn't faded. "You're a genius, Claire. Copper! Such a perfect name."

"HEY," THE TWINS SAID IN UNISON, but in very different tones.

They were identical and had an impeccable likeness to Dex, even having similar hairstyles as their eldest brother. They were about the same height as Claire, since they were so young, and were scrawny as a result of that as well. Their attitudes were very different, even at first glance.

Jorgen's only differing feature from Greg was his posture. His shoulders were slumped over, and his face was coated in an angst that only a teenager going through puberty could have. He glanced over at Naomi as if she were nothing more than another tree standing in the forest, his expression unchanging as he greeted her. Naomi could tell he wasn't happy about being here, and that was something that was rooted into his heart.

Unlike Jorgen, Greg had a bright smile on his face, his shoulders thrown back with pride as he said hello to Naomi. He had a natural charisma to him that shone through even with that one syllable word, like he genuinely wanted to say hello to her and not because he was being forced to by Claire. She could see that in his heart was great love and appreciation for the world, paralleled with an equal amount of naivety.

Naomi gave both of them a warm smile as Copper looped around them to sniff her. He let out a small growl that caused Naomi to jump.

"Copper, calm down, and be nice," Dex's voice bellowed out through the courtyard. He approached quickly, Copper meeting him halfway. "Scatter, boy," he pointed to the woods. Copper let out a small whimper before doing as his master commanded.

"Sorry about that, they don't take too well with new people," he said as he settled in between Claire and Greg.

Naomi put on fake smile and waved her hand nonchalantly as she said, "Oh, please, it's totally fine! I'm new, I understand."

Dex chuckled. "No need to fake it, they're terrifying."

Her smile didn't waver. "They're...majestic."

Claire laughed deeply. "Gods, don't be afraid to be honest about them. Dex and I were terrified when we met Fen for the first time. They're huge, wild animals."

Dex nodded. "You won't offend me by being honest. Even I'm scared of the bastards sometimes."

Claire smirked. Now Dex was lying to be nice, but she wouldn't rat him out.

"I'm going to the river," Jorgen muttered. He glanced at his twin, but Greg was focused on Naomi. Claire didn't miss his scowl before he slinked away. She couldn't help but feel bad for him. He wasn't adjusting too well, and that made her nervous. Especially now. Her heart squeezed as that thought washed over her. Someone was really going to die. No, it wouldn't be one of the guys, but one day it could be one of those charming little boys.

Vlad's hand on her arm drew her from her nervous musings, and she smiled up at him.

"Hey, Naomi! How are you doing?" Vlad said with a wide smile.

Naomi couldn't help but to smile back at him. "I'm doing well, yourself?"

He shrugged. "I'm always doing great."

Naomi really looked at his face for the first time. He had hooded, violet eyes, they were a different shade than Claire's, but had the same amount of vibrance. He had sandy brown hair that was tousled and messy. He had arched cheekbones with squared jaw and chin. He had a good heart, from what Naomi could see, and he was a genuinely happy person.

After they made small talk, Vlad lowered his head to whisper in Claire's ear. "Can I have a minute?"

EIGHT

The forest was unusually quiet as Claire and Vlad talked into the night. Everyone was on edge, even if they were on their best behavior. The magic felt a little off to Claire. Despite her demeanor, she was usually calm and collected. Now she just felt jumpy, as though she was hooked to a live wire.

"Who do you think it will be?" Vlad asked as they wandered through the woods. Everyone was on edge, and who could blame them? Someone's days were numbered.

Claire shook her head. "I have no idea."

Vlad turned suddenly, stopping her by placing a hand on her upper arm. "You're sure it's not you?" he asked, frantically searching her eyes.

"I promise it's not me," she said, taking one of his hands.

"It better not be. Naomi seems nice enough, but I'm not okay with you dying in her place."

Claire let out a laugh. "Stop! She's actually really nice. I think she'll fit in well."

"Is someone starting to warm up to the new girl?" Vlad joked.

"Everyone was kind of scared when they got here, of course she's no different. I'm going to play nice. Showing her around is only the right thing to do."

Vlad laughed as they continued to stroll through the forest.

"I don't know. The vision was very somber, it felt like it was foretelling something more than just the execution. There's something…more happening here," Claire said.

NAOMI WAS LAYING IN HER TEMPORARY BED, trying not to focus on the tension surrounding her. Even when she first arrived, things didn't feel like this. With every second that passed, the magic started to feel unbalanced. Vincent knocked on the door, startling her. She quickly composed herself and stood, calling him into the room.

"How are you doing?" he asked.

She shrugged. "I'm doing alright. How are you?"

"I'm handling everything okay. There's not too much time to think when I have to watch over a coven, which I'm thankful for." He gave her a sad smile.

"Everyone here has been really nice. You've raised them well," she joked.

"I learned everything I know from your mother. She was extraordinary."

Naomi gave him another somber smile as her stomach roiled at the memory of her mother's decaying corpse. "She was. I just wish we knew what happened."

Vincent sighed, his heart aching more, not that it had stopped since he heard the news. Knowing what killed her hurt even more.

"I'm tired of death already," Naomi whispered. "What's going to happen during the trial? Like, really? More than what you told the rest of the coven? You don't have to spare the details."

Vincent sighed. "Are you sure you want to know?" he asked, not sure that he really wanted to tell her.

"Yes," she said steadily.

He took a deep breath before speaking, thinking about his words carefully. "You will be standing in line with the other fourteen women in front of the table. Except, the table won't be like you normally see it. It'll be flat and raised a little off the ground, like a stage. One at a time, all of you will step up, and I will...evaluate you, in a way. Part of my abilities is to know the powers of every magical person, before they do sometimes, and see their potential power at maximum growth as well as where they are at now.

"My eyes will be pure white, just to warn you. They will glow with a brightness you've never seen before. After I have evaluated everyone, I will no longer have control. After that, I don't really know what happens yet... Something with air, since that's my affinity—"

"Affinity?" Naomi interrupted.

"Yes, everyone has an affinity for a certain element. Mine is air. Yours is water."

"Wait, if you can evaluate strengths, don't you already know who's going to...die?"

Vincent's face fell as he shook his head. "I have a hunch. I won't know for sure until the trial."

"I don't want someone to die for me, Dad."

"You won't die. You're nowhere near the weakest person here. In fact, you're one of the strongest. Haven't you been wondering why you're so much shorter than everyone, yet your eyes glow more intensely than mine sometimes?"

Naomi shrugged. "I haven't thought about it, honestly. I knew I was much shorter, but I don't see how that correlates with power. Or are you just saying this because you're my dad, and you'd sooner ruin the coven than kill me?"

He shrugged. "The world may never know, sweetheart."

"Wait—what's my power? You told me my affinity, but not my power."

He gave her a warm smile. "What have you always been good at?"

She thought for a long moment before waving her hands in defeat. "I have no idea."

"Reading people. And you've always been able to make me happy with just a smile."

"So this means what exactly?" she asked, voiced coated in confusion.

"You can read people's true...colors, if you will. You know what lies within them, and you can influence their feelings in any given

73

moment."

"Really? Is that why people look at me weird sometimes?"

He chuckled. "Yes, that's why I warned you to control your feelings when you got here. You're stronger than you think, sweetheart. I love you."

"I love you, too."

THE SOUND OF A BRANCH SNAPPING drew Claire and Vlad's attention away from one another. They were both on high alert, until they saw the figure appearing from the woods. "It's just Fen," Claire said unnecessarily.

Still, Vlad didn't relax. Claire approached Fen like she had so many times before, and Fen lowered his head so she could scratch behind his ear. She heard Vlad step closer, but what surprised her was Fen's reaction. He jerked his head up and snarled over Claire's shoulder, causing her to stumble backwards.

"Fen?" she asked, obviously alarmed. She hadn't seen him snarl at her since the day they'd found him. She said his name again, but he wouldn't look at her. He was staring intently—at Vlad, she realized. She turned her head, looking into Vlad's violet gaze. He didn't look scared, just concerned.

"Does he do this often?" he asked, not looking away from the snarling wolf.

"No," Claire whispered, trying to quell her fear.

For a moment, Fen backed down, his hackles lowering, and Claire thought they were in the clear. That was when he hunkered down and struck. Fen leapt over Claire and landed squarely on Vlad, knocking him to the ground. Vlad's hands lit up with flames, but there wasn't much he could do. He was pinned, and Fen, undeterred, looked like he was going for Vlad's throat.

Thinking quickly, Claire conjured a stone blade light enough to throw from her hand, without much effort. She wouldn't hurt Fen, but she had to get him away from Vlad. She threw the knife, aiming for Fen's shoulder blade, and it struck exactly where it was supposed to. Fen yelped and turned his attention to her, snarling savagely like he'd never seen her before. Claire couldn't help the tears that came to her eyes. This was Fen, and Fen was a part of Dex. How could this happen?

He started advancing towards Claire but stopped when fire started to snake up his hind leg, causing his attention to go back to Vlad.

"Stop!" she shouted, blood thundering in her ears. Vlad hesitated and the flames went out. That would cost him.

Unlike Vlad, Fen didn't hesitate and his massive fangs sunk into Vlad's leg. Flames shot out of his hands, igniting a few of the surrounding trees as he screamed in pain. Fen shook his head and tore a large portion of muscle out of Vlad's thigh.

Claire screamed Fen's name, begging him to stop. But he didn't. He was about to strike again. Tears blurred her vision as rocks started swirling around her hand. She flung the shards into Fen's back, doing her best not to hurt him too badly. Fen would recover from that. He had to. This time, Fen's rage-filled gaze locked onto her, and he charged.

Claire's arm went up as she tried to block her face from the attack. Fen seized her arm and started to tear at the flesh. Blood began to soak Claire's clothes and the heat of the flames around her caused sweat to dampen her brow. A shield of earth formed around her arm, blasting Fen back. Less than a second later, he was back on top of her, his teeth tearing into her arm again. Heart pounding against her ribs, Claire saw her life flash before her eyes. He was going to tear her arm off or worse—kill her. If he hurt her much more, she'd be dead no matter what. Injured coven members didn't last. Sobs racked her body as she looked into Fen's golden eyes. All she wanted was to see Fen in them, a perfect reflection of her best friend, but he wasn't there.

She whimpered his name as the stone sword took shape in her other hand. She wanted him to stop more than anything. If he just stopped she wouldn't have to do this. But he didn't stop. She screamed as she plunged the sword into his chest, causing him to drop her arm. He fell to the side, his weight leaving her body. Claire got to her knees in a daze, holding her torn arm to her side and jerked the sword out of his limp body.

NINE

DEX FELL TO HIS KNEES as a gut wrenching scream tore from his lips. He doubled over, clutching his chest as involuntary tears ran down his face. Blayne was suddenly next to him, her hand on his back. He shoved her off, trying to get to his feet, but he stumbled and fell. Dex, during his screams, felt an intense pain, but he couldn't explain where it was coming from. Screams left the other members of the coven as rock shards flew around, striking trees and hitting the cabins. Miraculously, no one was hit with the shards. He felt like part of him was dying...dying...*Fen!*

"What's wrong?" Farrah asked, rushing over to them.

"I don't know. He won't stop screaming," Blayne cried.

Farrah tried to touch Dex, but more shards flew out of him, striking her arm. She jerked back, tearing the fragment from her flesh before she healed herself. Not a moment later, Vincent emerged, controlled panic in his silver gaze.

"What's going on?" he barked, but no one answered.

When Fen's heart stopped beating, Dex felt it immediately. He felt like his heart had stopped as well. At least for a few moments. He stood and stared in the direction of his favorite familiar and started off in a run. He wasn't thinking clearly. He just needed to go.

Reality suddenly spun back into Claire's vision, and she looked down at herself. The sword was still in her hand. She didn't know where that strength had come from, probably adrenaline. She felt like she couldn't breathe. She was shaking horribly. She wasn't thinking. She wasn't... she wasn't...

Fen wasn't moving. He wasn't moving. Why wasn't he moving? Claire's mind was racing. She thought through what had just happened over and over again, trying to reassure herself of what she just did. She was trying to tell herself it was the right thing. It was the right thing, right? Right? She had no choice. She had no choice.

She finally heard the gut wrenching scream from someone in the direction of the coven. Claire didn't have to think twice about who it was.

She ripped part of her shirt off and pressed it into Fen's wound, trying to stop the bleeding. She knew he was dead, deep down, but she loved him. She killed him. She loved...killed...

She increased the pressure, causing more blood to pour out of her own wound. She finally glanced up to see Vlad, passed out and bleeding profusely. In a wave of pure desperation, Claire jumped away from Fen and landed next to Vlad. Fen wasn't alive. She couldn't help him. But if she didn't help Vlad, he would die, too. She didn't have an affinity for fire, but she could still use it. She used the heat to cauterize the wound, causing Vlad to wake up screaming with more flames shooting out from his hands, thankfully directed away from her.

"I'm sorry, I'm sorry," she chanted, but Vlad just kept screaming. She had to stop the bleeding. She had to… She looked a little to the right to see Dex running onto the scene, followed closely by Farrah and Vincent.

Her heart dropped to the center of the planet. The gravity of what happened finally hit her. Fen was dead. Fen attacked her. Fen attacked Vlad. Fen was going to kill her. She had no choice. She had…no…choice.

This was her best friend's family. This was *her* family. Her family... she killed...she loved…

Farrah used water to put out the fires raging around them. She took in the scene in front of her, her heart squeezing in her chest. Vlad was screaming, Fen was dead, and Claire's arm was wounded to the bone. Gods, what had happened?

Dex's face was twisted with rage and grief, rock spikes hovering around his whole body. He let out an enraged scream, the spikes starting to fly into the trees again. His heart squeezed when he finally saw Claire, hunched over Vlad. There was so much blood. But the blood on her was nothing compared to the blood all over Fen. His chest, back, and jaws were bathed in crimson and torn flesh. His fur was matted until he was unrecognizable. What was worse? Dex hadn't felt this until it was too late. He could have stopped this—if he had known. Why hadn't he known?

"What the *fuck* happened, Claire?!"

Her head snapped up as tears ran down her face. She stared at Dex, enraged and broken to the core. His dark blue eyes blazing with fury and emptiness—like part of him was gone. "Dex, you gotta believe—I loved—Dex, fuck, fuck, I'm so sorry, Dex."

Claire looked down at herself, still dazed and confused. She knew what she'd done, but she didn't have the words.

His stomach dropped as he realized what she was implying. "What *happened?!*" he screamed, more rocks flying into the trees.

"Dex, I'm so sorry. Dex. Fuck, Dex," she sobbed. She hadn't fully realized until that moment that she'd been crying.

Claire? Claire had done this to them?

He started to approach them, more rock shards surrounding him and racing around at an alarming rate. Vincent leapt in front of him, pinning him up against a tree. "Dexter, stand down!" Vincent yelled, waving his hand upwards. Suddenly all of Dex's rock shards disappeared as Vincent stunted his powers.

Farrah dropped down next to Claire, pulling her hands away from Vlad.

"He's still bleeding," Claire whimpered. All Claire saw was blood pouring out of someone's body. She had no idea that it was actually hers.

"Claire, sweetheart, look at me," Farrah said, pulling Claire's chin up to look into her eyes. "Vlad isn't bleeding. You are."

"I'm bleeding?" she asked, her wide eyes stared into Farrah's bright green ones.

Farrah didn't answer. Instead she lightly touched Claire's arm, causing Claire to scream. Before, she hadn't felt the pain of Fen's bite, but now she did. Shards would have flown out of her body, but Vincent was using his power to suppress all earth activity. Farrah would have to thank him for that later.

She examined the gouge in Claire's arm and winced. She had no idea how Claire was still conscious. She hovered her hand over Claire's wound, and it started to mend. She could only do so much, but Claire stopped screaming and for that, she was grateful. Once the bleeding had stopped and the wound was mostly closed, she dropped her hand and looked around. More coven members were starting to arrive.

"Blayne," Farrah barked, her voice uncharacteristically harsh. "Bandage Claire's arm."

Blayne obeyed without further prompt, and Farrah turned her attention to Vlad. His injury was far worse. Farrah knew that Claire would be okay. She would have scars, but she'd recover. Vlad, on the other hand, was missing an entire chunk of his thigh, femur exposed. Farrah could do a lot, but she couldn't regenerate flesh. As she did her best to mend what she could, she noted that Claire did a good job stopping the bleeding. She had to admire her courage, despite the circumstances. When she was done, Vlad's leg did look better, but he'd never walk without assistance again. That made Farrah feel sick. She knew enough about covens to know that this wound was a death sentence, one way or another.

"Get him back to his cabin," she ordered. Sam obeyed, easily lifting Vlad, and carrying him away.

They finally noticed the howling of the wolves—no, the crying of the wolves. Dru stepped forward to join Dex's side, staring at her fallen mate. She slowly stalked over to Claire, whose hands were still shaking, though her wounds were securely wrapped. Once she smelled the blood of her mate on Claire's body, she jumped back to her master's side.

Claire should have been scared of Dru, she would have every reason to hurt her. But she didn't have the energy to be scared. "They

79

have to save Fen," she croaked.

Blayne rubbed her back. "No one can save the dead," she said. "I'm sorry. I know how much he meant to you," she whispered, tears running down her own face.

Dex... Claire thought, looking over at him. He'd fallen to his knees and was leaning on Dru for support. Claire wanted to go to him, but she knew that wasn't a good idea. Vincent took Dex's arm and said, "Come on, let's get you out of here."

Dex violently shoved him off as he got back on his feet but still obeyed his commands, Blayne following close behind. Vincent followed him back to the coven, giving Farrah a sharp nod to tell her that she was in charge of the situation now.

"Claire, you have to tell me what happened," Farrah said.

She shook her head, her mind still racing with the same thoughts. She loved him. She killed him.

Farrah sighed, but understood. Claire was in shock and talking to her was useless for the time being. "Let's go back," she said softly.

Claire gave a lifeless nod and stood slowly with Farrah's support, leaning on her for the walk back to the coven.

Naomi came out from her temporary quarters through the table after the ruckus had quieted down to see Farrah bringing an injured Claire into the courtyard.

"Claire!" Naomi yelled, running to the both of them. "My gods, are you okay?"

Claire gave her a blank stare, so Naomi looked at Farrah who only shook her head quickly.

Naomi took a silent but deep breath and focused her energy on a serene feeling, projecting it towards Claire. She physically relaxed and gave Naomi a weak smile. "Thanks," she muttered.

"I can take it from here, Farrah," Naomi said.

Farrah gave her a quick nod. "I'm going to go check on Vincent and Dex." Instead of walking towards Dex's cabin, though, it looked like she was walking back towards the woods. Presumably to take care of Fen's body. Farrah would be able to heal the broken skin and clean up the blood before he was put to rest.

Claire leaned on Naomi as they finished the walk to her cabin.

"Do you want to relax? I can take you to your room," Naomi

offered.

Claire shook her head, still in a daze, and said, "Can you play that song again?"

Naomi walked her over to the couch, making sure Claire got settled okay before moving to the piano. While she started to play, she focused on emitting a calm feeling throughout the room. When the song finished, she glanced over at Claire, who had a more tranquil look on her face.

"Are you okay enough to tell me what happened?" Naomi asked, gesturing to her freshly-bandaged arm. Naomi knew something had gone terribly wrong when Vincent stormed out of his underground quarters to check on all the screaming, but he hadn't told her what, and he'd insisted that she stay behind.

Claire blinked back tears and fought another wave of dark emotion. She won that fight, thanks to Naomi's influence. "Vlad and I were walking around the woods when Fen just...fuck, Naomi, it was bad. He attacked Vlad, so I tried to stop him. I didn't think he would hurt me when I tried, but he bit my arm and...he wasn't stopping. He had to be stopped. I... He was going to kill me, Naomi. I have no idea why, either. I was there when Dex met him. The wolves love me, they've always been nothing but nice to me. I thought he would stop... I... Naomi, I didn't want to do it, I didn't, I loved him, and I... I loved him."

"Hey, stop," Naomi said softly, going to Claire's side. "You did what you had to do to survive. He was going to kill you. I know how much you loved them, and I've only been here a short time. Dex will understand." She started to emit more calming energy after seeing that Claire was getting riled up again.

Claire shook her head as a stray tear wandered down her cheek. "You haven't been here the past seven years, Naomi. Dex *loved* that wolf. Fen was his first familiar. They had months of bonding before the others showed up. Dex really grew up with him; we were sixteen when we met him. He was part of Dex. He... *we* loved him. You have no idea how much."

Naomi's heart squeezed in her chest, but she did her best not to focus on that sinking feeling. She had to keep her thoughts light and her energy calm. "I'm so sorry. That sounds so traumatic for the both of you. Does Dex know what happened?"

Claire's laugh was bitter. "I'm sure you heard his screams. They were impossible to miss. He was *so* angry. *So* angry. He's never going to forgive me. He's my best friend."

Naomi strengthened her calming energy again, wondering how much it would take to override Claire's anxiety and remorse. She already felt like she was at maximum capacity of her powers since she hasn't mastered them yet, but all she wanted was to make Claire feel better.

"You did what you had to do, Claire. You need to know that. Fen was going to kill you, and then probably Vlad right after. My dad would've had to take action if that happened, and gods know what he would do. It's probably a similar fate to what he already met. This wasn't your fault, Claire, and I'll be damned if you keep blaming yourself."

Claire paced the room, not knowing what to do. She just wanted go back an hour and fix everything. Fen shouldn't be dead, she shouldn't have lost Dex forever, and Vlad—at some point Vlad was going to die. Her entire world was falling apart, and there was nothing she could do about it. She did know one thing, though, she was glad that Naomi was with her. Her calming energy was the only thing keeping her sane. One day, when the world was back on it's axis, she'd have to repay her for that.

Claire gave her a small smile. "Thanks for trying tonight. I think... I think I just wanna sulk and sleep, though—if I can sleep."

Naomi smiled and gave her a slight nod. "I'll stick around out here, send good vibes, you know?"

TEN

NAOMI AWOKE IN UNFAMILIAR SURROUNDINGS. She glanced around for a few moments before realizing that she'd fallen asleep in Claire and Blayne's cabin the night before.

"Gods, what a night," she whispered to herself as she went through the events of the previous evening. She sat up slowly and started to make her way out of the cabin when Claire emerged from her room. Her eyes were almost swollen shut, and she looked like hell. She was covered in bruises, and her hair was damp. Now that all the dirt was gone, Naomi realized how horrible the fight had been.

"Hey, sorry I fell asleep here," she said.

Claire shrugged. "It's fine, I don't mind. Did Blayne come back?" she asked nervously.

Naomi shook her head. "Not that I noticed, at least. She might've just slipped in, and I slept through it," she said.

Claire nodded absently. Naomi started to glance around nervously, not really knowing what to say, when they both felt the familiar call of breakfast. It was always a magical tug that insisted you go outside, and you do so now. Claire didn't want to go outside. She didn't want to face her coven. She didn't want see Dex's broken face. She couldn't stand to see Vlad, if he was even there. Gods, would he be there? Claire had no idea. She'd gotten used to the idea that someone would die in the trial, but she never imagined that Vlad would die the second a new male arrived. The thought made her sick, but as the magical tug grew stronger, her resolve to deny it died.

"We have to go," Naomi whispered, her kind face full of dread.

Claire did her best to smile. "It's okay, Naomi. Let's go."

Naomi looked relieved to see that Claire was doing a little better, or maybe she was feeling numb. Either way, they left the cabin and subjected themselves to the harsh rays of the morning suns.

Every single coven member was quiet and sullen as they sat around the table. This breakfast was different. Usually, food was served right as everyone arrived, but today the surface was barren, and Vincent was absent. Claire's heart started to thud loudly against her ribs as she saw Dex's tall form move towards the center of the courtyard, followed closely by a subdued-looking Blayne, and Dru. But Dru didn't look quite right. Her fur was still snow white, but it didn't glisten and sparkle in the light like it was supposed to. Her icy, blue eyes were downcast as she walked next to Dex, and it looked as though every step took energy she just didn't have.

Claire couldn't keep watching. She just couldn't. She kept her eyes on her hands as she twisted them nervously in her lap. Claire glanced around, noticing that Vlad and Farrah were absent.

Naomi sensed the change in Claire's emotions, going from guilt to worry. She projected a feeling of warmth and serenity to Claire, at first, before realizing the whole coven needed that as well.

Once everyone was seated, Vincent emerged from Vlad's cabin. All eyes were on him as he walked to the table, drawing everyone's attention.

"After the events of last night, we must have another trial to settle internal matters before we can initiate the new coven member. Claire, please rise," Vincent said, voice booming.

Naomi's spine stiffened as she looked at Vincent, worry evident in her bright, blue eyes. He looked back at her for only a moment before shifting his focus back to Claire, who stood slowly in her spot next to Naomi.

"Will you please recount the events of last night?" he asked, unwavering.

Claire drew a shaky breath, not letting herself look at Dex as she spoke. "Vlad and I were in the woods last night and," Claire paused, her voice catching in her throat. "And Fen found us." She glanced at Vincent before cowering away from his silver gaze.

"What happened next?"

Claire swallowed, unable to help the silent tears that rolled down her cheeks or the way her hands shook. "Fen attacked Vlad," she said, her voice barely above a whisper. "I tried to get him to stop, he just…"

Dex shot to his feet, body rigid with pent up anger. "Fen wouldn't do that," he snarled. His eyes were a deeper blue than usual and their glow was stronger, more intense.

Claire flinched as though she'd been struck. She wanted nothing more than to run until she was far away. Back in Everton. Back in the orphanage. Away from all of this.

"Dex," Vincent barked, his voice amplifying. "Sit down."

As if pulled down by invisible ropes, Dex slumped on the bench, suddenly silent. Dru shifted uncomfortably, whining every once in a while and glancing towards the woods.

"What happened next?" Vincent repeated, turning his attention back to Claire. For a moment, Vincent regretted being a coven leader. When he'd first found Claire, she'd been scared, but she'd still had a fire about her. She'd been brave and headstrong. Now she was scared, yes, but she was also defeated and broken. He pushed those thoughts aside as he patiently waited for her answer.

"I threw shards at him," she said, her voice sounding less frail. "I knew those wouldn't really hurt him. He'd be fine in a couple of days. I thought he'd snap out of it, but he didn't. Instead, he just came for me. He didn't stop. I didn't have a choice." Her voice cracked on that last sentence, and her shoulders began to shake.

Dex shouted out again, "He wouldn't do that! I know my wolf."

"Dex! What did I say?" Vincent boomed. Naomi felt everyone's fear or anger in that moment, so she focused more of her power on calming everyone down.

Farrah emerged from Vlad's cabin, then. Her eyes were drained, evident that she'd spent the whole night trying to fix his leg. "We have thirty members right now," she said, her voice matching her eyes, "the magic is unbalanced. It's ripping at the seams. *No one* knew Fen last night. He was a wild animal, like he was before you were bound to him," she said to Dex.

The color drained from his face, but the anger he held didn't leave his eyes. "He was still Fen. None of you knew him like I did," he growled. The rest of Fen's pack started to appear in between the cabins, snarling.

"I did!" Claire yelled as he said it. "I loved him too! I was there when we met him. I was there for it all. And where the fuck were you, Dex? How could *you* not feel his emotions when he was trying to *kill me*?!" she sobbed.

The color drained from Dex's face, as if the truth had finally hit him. He stared at her, his ocean blue eyes wide as his hands shook. Copper emerged from the woods to stand at his mother's side. He whined and rubbed his muzzle against her shoulder. Dex's other wolves were visible just beyond the tree line, but they stayed silent. Dex finally shook himself and straightened. "Even if that's true, I'll never forgive you."

Vincent's voice boomed, "Farrah's point stands. The magic isn't balanced now. There are too many people here, the energy of the coven relies on balance and strength. We now have two members injured, one severely, a familiar is dead, we still have a trial. We have more important things to deal with. The trial will commence tomorrow. Claire, you were obviously acting out of self defense. Still, you committed a murder. One week, no powers. It will not hinder your chances tomorrow. Dex, you did not control Fen during his actions, but I will be watching you. If you get out of line, I will not think twice about punishing you as well. Eat and be on your way." Vincent turned and retreated to Vlad's cabin while Farrah sat down next to Claire.

"How's your arm feeling?" Farrah asked kindly, the tension leaving her face.

"It's okay. There's not any extreme pain. It just itches from the scab," Claire said, tears still streaming down her face.

Farrah nodded. "Good. Do you want to see Vlad? He's been asking for you."

Naomi squeezed Claire's arm and gave her a warm smile, "I'll leave you guys to it." She stood from the table and walked away.

Claire nodded at Farrah once Naomi had gone. "Please. How is he?" she asked, voice coated in worry.

Farrah sighed, "Best he can be. You know him, he's trying to remain positive."

They walked to Vlad's cabin. Upon entering, they saw Vincent pacing in the living room.

"Is it okay if I see him?" Claire asked Vincent.

He nodded. "Farrah, may I speak with you?" She stayed behind as Claire entered Vlad's room.

"Hey, good-looking," he said with a stiff smile.

"Hah, funny. How are you?" she asked, quickly moving to his side and grasping his hand.

"I'm doing positively fantastic. How are you?" he asked, the stiff smile never leaving his face.

"Oh, you know, the exact same," she said with much less enthusiasm. "Really, how are you?"

Vlad sighed, his usual optimism disappearing. "Farrah says I'll have to use a crutch for the rest of my life, but I'll heal…mostly. I'll live, I promise."

Her stomach dropped. She looked down at his leg, covered in gauze and bandages, and a wave of nausea overcame her. She snapped her head away, not being able to stand the sight. She did her best to smile at him, though. "As long as you promise," she said, tears falling again.

He lifted his hand to her face, and she placed her hand over his, giving it a squeeze. "Claire, stop that, please," he pleaded.

"It's my fault," she cried, "I'm the reason this happened. I should have stopped Fen."

"There was no stopping Fen. You did the right thing. He would have killed you, and then I would've had to kick his ass. He probably would've taken my other leg with him," he gave her a somber smile. He was always trying to make her laugh, and usually he was successful. Claire was full of too much despair to even smile.

"I can't believe this happened to you. You didn't deserve this," she said.

He sat up as best he could without moving his leg too much, and cupped his other hand around her cheek. "Claire, stop blaming yourself right now. Please. For me." He drew her face closer, kissing her softly. "Please," he begged.

She looked into his eyes. She leaned in this time and kissed him for a few moments. "I should go, let you get rest."

"Okay, if you insist. I'd much prefer if you stayed."

"I'm leaving you to get rest. I will see you later." She kissed the inside of his palm, still resting on her face, before removing his hands and walking out of the room.

All too soon, the moment of distraction was over, and that sinking feeling was back. The second Claire was back under the powerful rays of the suns, Naomi was at her side, emanating her power.

"Are you okay?" she asked.

Claire smiled, a little more genuine this time. "I'll be okay."

Naomi sighed and her eyes landed on Dex, who was fixated on Claire. They were full of pain, now, instead of pure rage. He lost his two best friends in one night. That realization was finally hitting him. His eyes moved to Naomi's before they shifted back to Claire. Naomi went rigid. She went to move between them, but Dex didn't move. Claire finally looked up and noticed what was happening. She started backing away from him, only stopped when she pressed up against a cabin. Seemingly out of nowhere, Dru was suddenly by her side. A sob wracked Claire's body, and she slumped to the ground, unable to support her own weight.

Dru's steady gaze stayed on Claire, watching her every move. That loving and trusting bond they'd shared had been shattered, and there was nothing anyone could do about it. Claire finally lifted her gaze to Dru. When their eyes collided, Claire felt her heart shatter into a million pieces. She saw nothing but pain in Dru's eyes, and Claire felt nothing but pain as she watched Dru walk away.

ELEVEN

NAOMI RAN TO CLAIRE'S SIDE, holding her hand out to help her up. "Come on, let's go inside." She led her to her cabin and shut the doors forcefully behind them.

Naomi focused her powers. "Are you okay?" she asked.

Claire's dazed look started to leave, thanks to Naomi. She didn't know what she would do without her in this situation. She shook her head, "Can we talk about you instead?"

Naomi looked startled. "Oh—sure. What do you want to know?"

Claire looked around the room, sighing, and her mind wandering. "Tell me more about Lakeshore," she said in a rush.

"Well, it's surrounded by gorgeous lakes. All the houses are intricate high-rises, but not like Everton. They're shorter and a lot farther apart. The different levels are all asymmetrical and not perfect like they are there. It's gorgeous at sunset, the suns reflecting off all the metal buildings. We had a perfect view of the sky as well. I had a personal balcony attached to my room. Every night I'd go out there and just stare at the stars with my friends, or sometimes alone, or with my parents. After Dad left, we did that a lot," she reminisced, her eyes staring off into nothing as she pictured the scene in her mind. It was directly followed by an image of her mother's face, shriveled and grey on the kitchen floor. Her face drained, and she snapped back to look at Claire.

"I didn't ask for this, you know," Naomi said suddenly. "I didn't want to be the first one to come here and ruin everything you guys had. I wanted to be with my family again, but not under these circumstances."

"I know, it's okay. None of us blame you. This is just how coven life is," Claire said. It felt good to talk about someone else's internal issues. It was distraction. Claire needed all the distraction people were willing to give. She was also happy to be there for Naomi, who'd given so much to her already.

"I understand that. I just hate being this person who is causing so many problems," she said softly.

"No one blames you. Not one person. Not for anything. Anyone could have walked in here, and the same thing would have likely happened. This is not directly because of you," she said sternly.

"Claire, my mother died," she spat. A few empty tears started to roll down her face. She wanted so much to tell someone what happened to her mother—she'd wanted so much to tell *Claire* what happened to her mother.

"What?" Claire asked, completely astounded.

"I came home, my last day in Lakeshore, to find her. She was in the kitchen, making dinner, when *something* sucked the life out of her. That's the only way I know how to describe it. She was shriveled, grey, and her hair was falling out. Her clothes looked like they never would have fit her. Something had to have done that to her, I just can't wrap my mind around what... who could do that to her? She was innocent, and never did a thing wrong. She was nothing but loving to anyone who came near her. I found her laying there when I was drawn to the coven. I was forced to leave her there. I couldn't even say goodbye."

Claire's jaw dropped. She had no clue Naomi's pain stemmed from her mother's death, not just from leaving her behind. Her story sounded familiar, in a way, before something clicked in Claire's mind. "That's how my parents died. I—I faintly remember seeing them in the same way you describe before I was taken to the orphanage."

"You're an orphan?" Naomi asked, dumbfounded.

"It's okay, it happened when I was very young. I didn't register what happened to them until you said that. Does Vincent know who... what did this?"

Naomi shook her head, her eyes clearing up. "I told him what happened just as I arrived, and he didn't let on like he knew what was capable of that. He seemed just as distraught as I was."

"There has to be some way to figure out what happened," Claire said softly.

Naomi laughed bitterly. "I don't know. I don't know because the moment I found her, the coven dragged me here."

Claire's heart broke for Naomi in that moment. To be torn from her mother's body only moments after finding her dead must have been gut wrenching. "Coven magic has a funny way of doing things like that."

"That doesn't make me feel better."

Claire gave her a wry smile. "I didn't think it would." They sat in silence for a few moments before a wide grin spread across Claire's face. "Do you want to see something cool?"

TWELVE

TODAY WAS THE DAY. The weight of the last few days hadn't lifted completely, but there was a clarity in the damp, morning air. The day passed slowly without much activity. Coven magic was something Claire would always struggle to explain. Though she was certain she'd make it out alive, she had no idea who would die. Nothing from her vision had been clear. Not hair color nor eye color, though she was pretty sure it hadn't been bright red, so she was confident that May would be okay. Still, Claire felt sick as dinner came to a close. No one had eaten much of anything. Which of course made sense. How did you eat when you knew that either you or one of your friends would certainly meet their demise?

Dex reluctantly looked at Claire. Her violet eyes had dark circles underneath them, and they seemed less vibrant. There was grief and worry painted across her sharp features. Claire was injured and the implications of that finally sank in. Farrah had said that she would fully recover, but she was still wounded. Whether she would recover or not, being weak at a trial was never good. That thought made him feel sick. He might be angry with Claire beyond belief, but he didn't want her dead. Next to him, Blayne was practically vibrating with nerves. She'd been glued to his side every minute since the attack. An attack that Dex still couldn't explain. Well, Farrah had said that the magic in the coven went haywire until the new member was properly inducted. If that was true, that meant this could have been prevented if they'd just done the trial right away—not that the magic would have allowed that. Or if he hadn't been weak. Somehow, his control had snapped, and his first familiar was dead. His stomach roiled when her gaze briefly met his. She quickly glanced away, but that didn't stop his heart from racing.

Vincent slowly rose to his feet, looking out at the faces of his coven. This would be just the first of many times he would have to do this, but nothing could really prepare him to execute someone. Still, it had to be done. It was the way of the covens and waiting had caused so much turmoil already, though he didn't have a choice. The magic dictated the timeline. He did not.

Naomi squeezed Claire's hand in a vice-like grip as she saw her father rise. Her heart pounded in her chest as the guilt assailed her. She wasn't ready to watch someone die, and she really wasn't ready to watch someone die because of her.

"It is time," Vincent said, his voice rolling over everyone with immense power.

They hadn't been briefed on the exact ceremony, yet everyone knew to stand and back away from the table. Naomi and every current female member lined up in front of the table while seven male members flanked to the left and the other seven flanked to the right. As Vincent stepped onto the table top, it shifted and changed beneath his feet, becoming a stage rather than a place to have meals. Naomi was nervously wringing her hands and fighting back tears. All around them, torches rose from the ground, igniting on their own as invisible shackles wrapped around their ankles. The sudden flood of light and heat gave Claire goosebumps. It wasn't dark, but it would be soon. The extra light made it look like the suns were still high in the sky. Claire didn't think that was how torches usually worked, but she was standing in front of a magic table, after all.

Vincent blinked once and when he opened his eyes, they were white and glowing brighter than anything Claire had ever seen. Her breath caught, and if it weren't for the magic holding her in place, she would have backed away.

"For one of you, your time ends here," he said. Only, it didn't sound like his voice. It was deeper than usual and it sounded like there was more than one of him talking.

For Vincent, there was dark nothingness, like he was asleep. He'd remember it when he came to, but for now, nothing but the magic was in control. "Your time at the coven is over, but your memory and magic will live on forever."

A shiver ran down Claire's spine. Something was off with Vincent. The words were coming out of his mouth, but they weren't his. They were the product of magic so powerful, it was palpable in the air around them. The first person in line was Farrah, and, for once, she actually looked scared. Usually, nothing phased her calm and dainty expression. It seemed that death was the one thing that could. When Vincent's eyes locked on hers, a shudder went through her body. Claire held her breath, hoping and praying to whatever gods were listening that Farrah wouldn't die. Finally, the wave of power holding Farrah hostage left and Vincent's eyes left her. The same happened with the next two women, then May, and then Vincent's eyes were on Claire. Claire took a moment to appreciate that the other two women closest to her would be okay. Thank the gods.

Naomi watched as her father examined Claire. A lump formed in her throat as something new happened. A slight glow formed around Vincent's whole body and it pulsed like a heart beat. *Please don't let that be bad*, she thought desperately.

Knowing that Farrah, May, and the two others were safe, Dex could focus on Claire. When he saw the pulsating light coming from Vincent's body, Dru, who was across the courtyard, whined. He hadn't meant to send his churning emotions to her, but he couldn't help it.

Claire was fascinated by the glow permeating Vincent's body, but it didn't scare her. Despite recent events, Claire's visions hadn't changed, and they'd never been wrong before. Claire might be executed by Vincent one day, but today wasn't that day.

Naomi sighed in relief when she saw her father move away from Claire. They hadn't known each other long, but she didn't think she could handle it if Claire had been the one to die.

Dru let out a relieved whimper and slumped to the ground once Dex knew for sure that Claire was safe. He hated himself for feeling this way, but as long as it wasn't Claire, he didn't give a damn who died in Naomi's place.

Next in line was Naomi. The same thing happened, only more intense. Claire's heart raced as she watched until Vincent finally looked away from her and shifted his focus to Blayne.

Blayne's heart felt like it stopped in her chest when the glow from Vincent's eyes poured out and coated his entire body. His right hand extended, and she saw he held a silver handle detailed with intricate designs. She jumped when a blade made of pure air extended from the hilt. She wanted to scream, but she could do nothing as she was yanked forwards onto the stage.

Claire's eyes went wide as she met Blayne's wild gaze. The second Vincent's hand grabbed hers, the light in her hazel eyes went out, and Naomi stumbled backwards, clutching her face. A block slowly rose out of the stage, making no noise as everyone stared in horror. Finally, Blayne found her voice.

"No!" she screamed, and wrenched her arm, trying to break Vincent's grip.

"Silence," he commanded, still with that unearthly tone that wasn't his.

Blayne was frozen. Stuck inside her own head. She couldn't move. Vincent had done this to her. He'd trapped her. He was going to kill her. She was his prisoner. She dropped to her knees in front of the block. Her heart was racing, but no outward signs of panic were showing.

Claire was stunned by how subdued Blayne looked. One word from Vincent, and she was as calm as ever.

The seconds ticked by in painful silence as Blayne waited. She wanted to run. Wanted to scream. Wanted to escape. But there was no escape.

"You have served your coven well," Vincent's many grating voices said over the heavy silence.

Blayne's breathing picked up and her pulse pounded in her neck as Vincent lifted his sword and it arced down in one, swift motion.

ABOUT THE AUTHORS

Adaline McMillan grew up in Georgia where she found her passion for writing and editing. In addition to her pursuits as an author, Adaline is also pursuing a Bachelor of Science in Art Marketing and a Master of Fine Arts.

Teressa J. Martin is a published author currently residing in Atlanta, Georgia.
Insert author bio text here Insert author bio text here Insert author bio text here Insert author bio text here Insert author bio text here